hangman'

FRANK PERETTI

hangman's curse

THE VERITAS PROJECT

Tommy nelson™
Thomas Nelson, Inc. • Nashville

HANGMAN'S CURSE

Published in Nashville, Tennessee, by Tommy Nelson®, a division of Thomas Nelson, Inc.

Library of Congress Cataloging-in-Publication Data

Peretti, Frank E.
    Hangman's Curse / written by Frank Peretti
      p. cm. — (The veritas project ; #1)
    Summary: When several students at Baker High School are stricken by an alleged curse of the school's ghost, Elijah and Elisha Springfield and their parents, undercover investigators, are sent to uncover the truth behind the events.
    ISBN 0-8499-7616-2
    [1. High schools—Fiction. 2. Schools—Fiction. 3. Bullies—Fiction. 4. Christian life—Fiction. 5. Mystery and detective stories.] I. Title. II. Series.

PZ7.P4254 Han 2000
[Fic]—dc21

00-045084

Printed in the United States of America
01 02 03 04 05 BVG 9 8 7

Contents

Interoffice Memo

To: The President
        The White House
        Washington, D.C.

From: Mr. Morgan

Per your request, please be advised that we have assembled an independent investigative team, a family by the name of Springfield, consisting of both parents and their twin children, a boy and a girl. As you can see from the attached file, these people have extensive training and experience in crime prevention and investigation and are well qualified to fulfill the stated mission requirements: to investigate and solve strange mysteries, crimes, and occurrences, seeking not only the Facts, but the Truth behind the Facts, and to report their findings and suggestions.

Since, as you have requested, the team will be operating from a biblical, Judeo-Christian perspective, the team will be funded through private, non-tax-deductible contributions and will have no connection with or support from the government or your administration.

However, as you have requested, you will have input in choosing each assignment for the team, and will receive a written report from the team upon the completion of each assignment.

Considering the mission description for the team, we thought of the Latin word for truth, veritas, and have code-named this effort The Veritas Project.

We have placed articles and advertisements in selected print media and are already receiving requests for assistance. I will bring the first batch of requests to your office at your earliest convenience.

Morgan

1

APPOINTMENT
WITH FEAR

BAKER HIGH SCHOOL quarterback Jim Boltz wiped his hands on his jersey, angrily this time. He'd almost fumbled the snap again, the third time in the first quarter. His hands were slick with sweat. They were shaking. He clenched them into fists.

"Y'okay, Jim?" asked the center.

"M'okay!" he snapped back.

He was looking bad; he knew it and his team knew it. He had to get it together, had to quit missing, dropping, forgetting. This was an important game, Baker against Whitman. The Baker High School stadium was filled to capacity. He took his place in the huddle, his stomach in knots.

"Okay, uh, double-wide right, tight end left, 755 fly, on one. Ready . . ."

"We just did that play," said Dave, one of the wide receivers.

Jim stared at the turf. He was thinking about breathing.

Howie suggested, "How about power-I right, play action 242 . . ."

Jim's brain finally snapped into gear. "Uh, yeah, yeah, uh, tight end down and out, on two. Ready . . ."

"Break!" they all yelled.

The huddle broke and they headed for the line of scrimmage.

Jim forgot the play. He tagged his fullback and got a reminder.

"Ready, set, red twenty-one, red twenty-one, red twenty-two, hut, *HUT!*"

He got the snap, faded back, looked for his receiver, saw a face in the stands . . . The face was pale. The eyes were cold and cruel, and they gazed at him unblinkingly.

Jim's hand trembled. He almost dropped the ball.

ૹ

"Why's he standing there?" Coach Marquardt growled from the sidelines. Still in his midtwenties, Marquardt was all meat, no fat, and tough enough to scare any kid within range of his glare. "Boltz! Wake up and throw the ball!"

ૹ

Jim threw the ball. It wobbled in a pitiful, lazy arc over the line of scrimmage and bounced far short of the receiver. The play was over, and it was sheer luck the ball wasn't picked off by a linebacker.

This time, Gordon, the center, got right in his face. "Jim, what's the problem? Hey, I'm talking to you!"

Jim was eyeing that face in the stands. "Sleazy little wimp!"

The center turned to follow Jim's gaze. "Who?"

"He's gonna pay for this."

Gordon was still looking. "Who?"

Jim turned toward the huddle. "C'mon." It was fourth down on Whitman's 24-yard line and Baker had four yards to go for a first down.

Jim took some deep breaths. It had to be exhaustion. Maybe it was the stress of playoffs coming up. With two more wins, they'd go to the state championship game on Turkey Day, the big one. That could be doing it. Maybe it was a touch of the flu, or something he ate. It could be anything.

Anything but—

Fear.

Uh-uh. No way. Not me, not here, not now, and not from that little creep in the stands. He looked at those distant black eyes and mouthed the words, *I'm not afraid of you!*

കൈ

Ian Snyder sat hunched like a vulture in row twelve on the far end of the bleachers, dressed in black, the only color he owned. The seats all around him were vacant. After three miserable years in high school, he was used to it. He was enjoying every moment of watching Baker High's star quarterback fall apart. The searing, demonic smile never left his face. *Oh, you're scared, all right. I can see it in the way you keep looking this way and keep blowing this football game. I've got you right where I want you, don't I?*

"Abel Frye," he whispered, his eyes gleaming like the silver pendant that hung from his left ear. "Abel Frye."

⊘ᴚ◌

Jim Boltz shook off the weakness, clamped his hands together to keep them steady, and called for one more pass play, a last-ditch attempt to make that first down.

The Baker Hawks went to the scrimmage line; he took the snap, faded back—

His arm faltered in midthrow.

Someone was standing in the end zone.

Abel Frye. The name reverberated like an iron bell through his brain, taking command of every thought, every intent, numbing every nerve.

Beneath the upstretched arms of the goalpost stood a gaunt, decaying figure washed pale by the floodlights, shreds of a tattered shirt moving like vapors in the breeze, the head cocked grotesquely against the right shoulder as if the neck were broken, a golden-eyed hawk perched on the left shoulder. The youth looked dead, his face a chalky white, and yet his eyes met Jim's and then his pale, gray lips parted in a hideous grin.

They knew each other. This was an appointment.

⊘ᴚ◌

"YES!" said Ian Snyder, leaping to his feet, arms high in jubilation. Those who noticed had no idea what he was so excited about.

⊘ᴚ◌

The hawk's wings burst open as it leaped off the bony shoulder. With head low and eyes crazed with killing, it came straight for Jim Boltz.

Every thought fled from Jim's mind. He had no awareness of the game, the football in his hand, or the opposing tacklers breaking through. The only reality for Jim Boltz was fear.

Searing, mind-conquering fear.

The hawk grew larger as it came closer, wings beating furiously, talons open.

Jim Boltz turned and ran.

ᘓᐧᘔ

Coach Marquardt came unglued and almost crossed the sideline onto the field. "What in Sam Hill is he doing? BOLTZ! TURN AROUND!"

Assistant Coach Raddison could only gawk, but he did put a hand on Marquardt's shoulder in the hope of containing his temper.

The hawk's wings burst open as it leaped off the bony shoulder. With head low and eyes crazed with killing, it came straight for Jim Boltz.

Their star quarterback was outrunning Whitman's tacklers, running faster than they'd ever seen him run, but in the wrong direction. The Baker crowd was on its feet, roaring, shrieking, waving, trying to get Boltz's attention. The Whitman crowd was on its feet as well, but hysterical, pointing, laughing, having a great time.

Jim's receivers reached the end of their patterns, turned, and then stood there, bewildered and incredulous as their quarterback shrank in the distance and both teams fell into confusion.

Coach Marquardt signaled "time out" and crossed onto the field, cursing and fuming.

Raddison grabbed his arm. "Vern, the play isn't over!"

"*What* play?" Marquardt jerked free. "It's happening again. Can't you see that? BOLTZ! I'm gonna put your rear in a blender! You hear me?"

Raddison saw Jim Boltz collapse and roll into the end zone, get to his feet again, collapse again. The ball tumbled free and a Whitman tackler dove on it. The referee blew his whistle and the play was over.

Raddison had seen this before. "Oh, no." He hollered, "First aid! Let's go!" and then ran after Marquardt.

"TIME OUT!" Marquardt hollered, signaling, and he got it.

೧⊙

A Whitman tackler trotted up to the Baker quarterback, still on the ground. "Hey, congratulations, you just got us two points!"

The quarterback was writhing on the ground, whimpering, screaming. "What dollar in the kenzo slater, make it uptown and drive it, down way!"

The tackler had extended his hand to help his opponent off the ground, but now he shied back. "Hey, you all right?"

Boltz was twitching, twisting, staring wide-eyed at nothing and plainly terrified. "Does it, does it, no, unload and white the ground! Chevy maker in the postgame!"

He threw up his arms as if fending off an attack from . . . something.

"Wow," said the tackler to a teammate, "he's, he's—"

"He's wacko, that's what he is."

"Abel Frye!" Boltz screamed, inching and clawing along the ground, eyes staring upward. "Abel Frye!"

Then he was on his feet, starting to run.

Marquardt and Raddison overtook him and brought him to the ground, holding him down, trying to contain his lashing arms and kicking feet.

"Give us a hand here!" Raddison shouted, and players from both sides came to help hold Jim down.

"Where's the doc?" Marquardt shouted, searching. Then he slapped Jim Boltz on the helmet. "Cut it out, Boltz!"

A medic came running, emergency kit in hand.

The field was filling with parents, schoolmates, fans, the curious.

"Please stay off the playing field," said the announcer over the loudspeakers. Nobody listened.

The medic took charge. There was no need to check for pulse or breathing; the poor kid had plenty of both. "Let's get him inside. Careful, now."

"Make way there!"

Marquardt was on one arm, Raddison on the other. Between them, Jim Boltz began to weaken, his voice ebbing from a scream to a whimper. As they reached the passage to the locker rooms, his head began to droop and he muttered two last words before he passed out: "Abel Frye . . ."

Marquardt cursed and looked at Raddison.

Raddison nodded grimly. "You're right. It's happening again."

&

As the puzzled and murmuring football crowd gravitated toward the field, Ian Snyder turned and stole quietly up the stairs to the exit, his hands in the pockets of his long black trench coat. *Yeah,* he thought, *now Boltz will be just like the others.* In all the confusion, no one gave his presence in the stands a second thought.

&

In Washington, D.C., far from the Capitol dome, was an old red-brick office building with office space and apartments available for rent. On the fifth floor, at the end of a narrow hall with a noisy steam radiator, was a plain little office with its title painted in small black letters on the door: The *Veritas* Project. Just inside that door, Consuela, the secretary, sorted through conventional mail at her desk. Seated at a computer nearby, Carrie, the assistant, scanned through e-mails from all around the country. Between their two workstations was another door, and beyond that door was the cluttered office of Mr. Morgan, the boss.

Mr. Morgan was sitting at his cluttered desk, his suit jacket draped over the back of his chair, his tie loosened, his shirt sleeves rolled up. He was reading a field report he'd just received via the Internet: "Springfield/Montague/Phase Two." What he read pleased him, and he smiled, nodding his head.

Morgan was middle-aged, bald, bespectacled, and generally unimpressive in appearance. His name and face were not widely known in this town, and his office was in an obscure, hard-to-find location. He preferred it that way. A project like *Veritas* could benefit from being quiet, unknown, and behind-the-scenes. He was well connected with the *right* people, and that was all that mattered.

His telephone bleeped and the voice of his secretary said, "Mr. Morgan, the President on line one."

He picked up the receiver, pressed the button for line one and responded, "Mr. President."

The voice on the other end was immediately recognizable. Mr. Morgan was hearing from the foremost leader of the free world. "Mr. Morgan, I understand we have trouble brewing in Baker, Washington."

"Yes, sir. I heard from the high school counselor just this morning."

"Mr. Gessner."

"Yes. So you've read my report already?"

"Every word of it. And I agree. *Veritas* should have a look at it. Where are the Springfields now?"

Mr. Morgan glanced at the report he'd just finished reading. "Montague, Oregon. That drug abuse prevention program."

"How long before they're finished with that?"

Mr. Morgan looked at his watch. "Well . . . it could be as soon as half an hour, if everything goes according to plan."

ℰℱ

In a quiet old neighborhood where ancient maple trees overshadowed the street with their shady branches and pushed up the sidewalks with their roots, where the yards were small and neat except for an occasional neglected bicycle or forgotten skateboard, a late-model station wagon pulled slowly to a stop along the curb.

Inside, the driver looked warily at the gabled gray house several doors down the street. "That's it." He was a high school kid, sixteen or seventeen, thin, and nervous. Beside him sat another high schooler, a girl. Neither appeared to have slept, eaten, or bathed in days, and both were dressed in weird, pricey clothing that carried the same message as their dour expressions: Let the whole world drop dead.

In the rear seat, a young man with a grim, wary expression peered out the window and asked, "Are they ready?"

"If they aren't ready for company we won't get through the front door," said the driver. "I called 'em and they said it was all clear."

"So let's do it."

They got out of the car and crossed the street quickly, while looking up and down the street and toward the surrounding houses in case anyone might be watching.

An unkempt, slightly heavy blond woman in jeans and over-sized shirt answered the front door on the third knock. She recognized the boy and girl. "Hey, Luke. How you doing, Leah?" She eyed the stranger warily. "This must be Marv."

"This is Marv," Luke confirmed. "The buyer I told you about."

She studied Marv's face, her suspicion never waning. "How long have you known him?"

"We buy from him all the time. He's okay," said Leah.

The woman flung the door open. "Well, come inside before somebody sees you."

They walked into a modest living room. The carpet was worn, with several years' worth of cigarette holes. The furniture looked old, smelled old, and nothing matched. A big cat lay curled on the couch and looked up at them for only a moment before lowering its head again in disinterest.

"Let's see your money," said the woman. "Convince me."

Marv reached into his pocket and pulled out a thick wad of bills. "You're not dealing with a small-timer."

She was impressed at the sight of the hundred-dollar bills. "So Luke and Leah tell me." Her expression softened. "I'm Nancy.

My husband Lou's down in the lab right now."

He smiled, only slightly. "So let's see your goods. We'll make this quick."

He followed her into the kitchen where she reached into a drawer and produced a plastic bag containing white powder. "One hundred grams of crank, finished up just this morning."

Now it was Marv's turn to be impressed. "You must have some kind of lab."

"We don't talk about it."

He started counting out the big bills. "I'll take it."

"You'll take half. The rest is spoken for."

"Okay, half."

"We gotta go," said Luke. "If I get caught skipping class one more time, somebody's gonna get wise."

"Go out the back way," she instructed. "Use the alley."

The two kids ducked out the back, leaving Nancy and Marv alone to close the drug deal.

"So, fifty grams," said Nancy, taking a triple-beam balance from a cupboard.

"Wow," said Marv, "nice scale." Then he noticed the "SCHOOL DISTRICT 212" label still attached to the side and chuckled.

She smiled. "I have friends in the school district."

He boasted, "So have I. I work Mannesmann High, Cleveland, Kennedy, Lincoln Junior High, even Dwight Elementary."

She raised her eyebrows. "You do get around." She placed a coffee filter on the scale and began carefully pouring out the powder, watching for the scale to tip at fifty grams. "So how come I never heard of you before?"

"I'm smart," he replied. "How come I never heard of *you* before?"

She stopped pouring. She had fifty grams. "I'm smart, too."

She carefully poured the powder into a bag, then waited for Marv to place the hundred-dollar bills in her hand. When he did so, she gave him the bag.

"Thanks," he said. "It'll take about a week to sell this, and then I'll—"

There was a commotion on the back porch. A door banging open. Stumbling footsteps. An angry voice.

Marv was about to bolt for the front door, but Nancy said, "It's Lou."

The back door burst open and the two high schoolers stumbled into the kitchen, shoved along at gunpoint by a big, stubbly-faced man.

"Lou!" said Nancy. "What gives?"

Lou shoved the two kids up against the counter and then

The back door burst open and the two
high schoolers stumbled into the kitchen,
shoved along at gunpoint by a big,
stubbly-faced man.

growled in a roughneck, East Coast accent, "Found these two outside, snooping through the kitchen window with *these!*" He threw a tiny video camera and a set of earphones on the kitchen table.

Nancy looked at the gadgets, then at the kids, in horror. "We heard a rumor about some kids working undercover. It's *you?*"

Lou pointed the gun at Marv. " 'kay, Marv—or whoever you are—party's over. Better join your friends." He motioned with the gun toward the frightened Luke and Leah.

"What are you talking about?" said Marv, half raising his hands.

"They brought you here with 'em, and guess what? They're working for the cops. That means *you're* working for the cops."

Marv was totally flustered. "No, man, I don't know anything about this."

Nancy's eyes were suddenly cold and cruel. "You were good. Real good. You had us fooled!"

"But, but I'm not with them!" Marv protested.

Lou came closer, raising the gun to the level of Marv's eyes. "Oh, riiiight, like I don't know a sting operation when I see it? Open the jacket. You're probably wired."

Marv spread his jacket open. "No! No wires! No microphones, nothing! I'm clean, I tell you. I don't know these kids."

Lou was insulted. He spoke sideways to Nancy, "He says he don't know 'em!"

"I mean—"

"You drive up with 'em, you come into the house with 'em, and you don't know 'em? Eh, give me a break!"

Nancy glared at Marv in murderous rage. "So what are we going to do, Lou?"

Lou grabbed the video camera and earphones off the table, dashed them to the floor, and shattered them under his heel. He grabbed Leah by the arm as she screamed in pain, then aimed the gun at her. "How much do the cops know? How much have you told 'em?"

She didn't answer, but only squirmed in his iron grip, her face contorted with pain.

"Let her go," Luke blurted. "We haven't told them anything. We were supposed to take the recording back to the drug task force." Then he added with a tone of warning, "And if they don't hear from us within an hour they'll come looking for us."

"Elijah," the girl screamed, "don't tell them that!"

Lou nodded, a sly smile forming on his lips. "Hey, that gives us time, doesn't it *Elijah?* So what's *your* name, sweetheart?"

"Elisha." She pronounced it Eleesha. "Elisha Springfield."

"So Elijah must be your brother."

Elijah confessed, "That's right."

Lou smiled menacingly. "So it's all in the family." He waved the gun at Marv. "So who's this, your cousin?"

"You gotta believe me," Marv pleaded. "I'm not with them! I'm just here to do business!"

Lou aimed the gun in his face and pulled the hammer back. "You got two seconds to convince me."

"Jackie Morelli, over in the central district—you can call him. He knows me."

Lou shook his head. "Don't know him."

"Eddie Baylor? Runs Hogie's Tavern over on Torrance Boulevard."

Lou was unimpressed. "You gotta be making this up."

Marv was getting desperate. His voice was rising in pitch and he was talking a lot faster. "Okay, okay. Jimmy Dorning, over at—"

"Where are you getting these *nobody* names?"

"Just let me finish! He lives right next to Lincoln High School. He's my contact over there and we've made good money—I'm talking thousands, tens of thousands, and no rip-offs."

Lou cocked his head slightly as if he were just beginning to believe. "What about Steve Vernon? You know him?"

"I know him. I don't like him, but I know him. He's buying from Gomez and trying to get Gomez to cut me out."

Lou raised one eyebrow as if impressed. "You know Gomez?"

"Yeah, you kidding? Everybody knows Gomez."

"You work for him?"

Marv hesitated to answer. Lou brought the muzzle of the gun a little closer. "I don't ask questions twice, kid."

"Okay! Okay!" Marv finally burst out. "I work for him!"

"How long?"

"A year. Maybe two."

"How'd you meet up with him?"

"He helped me out."

"Yeah, just like all his little flunkies. So where's his lab?"

"He has an old rental on Taylor Avenue."

Lou's grip on the gun tightened. "He's at his *mother's* place!"

"No, no, no!" Marv raised his hands pleadingly. "He moved just last week! Go ahead, check it out! 401 Taylor Avenue!"

"So if you work for Gomez, why are you buying from us?"

"Because . . ." Marv couldn't finish.

"You're setting us up!"

"NO! NO! I just . . . I just gotta get away from Gomez, that's all." Marv began to wilt. "I can't take it anymore."

"So go home."

Marv seemed close to tears. "Don't have the bread. Gomez takes it all."

Lou eyed Marv curiously. "You mean, you do all the selling, but Gomez takes the money?"

"That's the deal. He puts me up, gives me a bed, maybe some food, and I work for him."

Nancy's voice was almost compassionate. "Dealing drugs just to stay alive. So what happens to Gomez if you get caught?"

Marv shrugged. "I dunno. Says he doesn't know me, I guess."

Lou sniffed in disgust. "Some friend."

Marv wiped a tear from his eye. "Yeah. Some friend. I'm just trying to get out on my own, that's all. I wouldn't even cut in on Gomez's turf. I'd go somewhere else. I just need something to get started, you know?"

Lou thought it over for several torturous seconds. Finally, he relaxed and raised the muzzle of the gun toward the ceiling. "Okay, Marv, okay. I guess you do know some people."

CRASH! The front door caved in and the house filled with green-jacketed, helmeted police, all leveling guns. "FREEZE! POLICE! ON THE FLOOR! ON THE FLOOR! GET DOWN! SPREAD 'EM!"

Nancy screamed, Lou dropped his gun, the kids fell to the floor and cowered. Marv ran for the back door, but Elijah Springfield hooked his feet in a leg lock and brought him down. More cops came storming in the back door, yelling, shoving, grabbing, flipping Marv over, holding him down, cuffing him. "DOWN! DOWN! DOWN! C'MON, MOVE IT!"

They slapped handcuffs on Lou and Nancy, then on Elijah and Elisha. In mere seconds, all five were facedown on the floor, subdued and guarded by the armed police now towering over them.

An officer found the fifty grams of methamphetamine in the pocket of Marv's jacket. They took him first. With a huge officer grabbing him under each arm, he sailed up from the floor and through the house before he could even get his feet under him. He went out through the front door, the sweeping blue and red lights of the police cars flashing across his dazed face, and then he was gone.

The door slammed shut.

"Don't move," a burly sergeant warned the others.

Lou and Nancy didn't move. They just waited. Elijah and Elisha remained on their bellies, looking even more dour than usual.

Outside, the doors of a police car slammed shut and the vehicle sped away, its lights making one final sweep through the living-room windows. Seconds later, a police officer poked his head in the door and said, "Suspect is en route."

Lou and Nancy, still facedown and handcuffed, smiled at each other.

Elijah sighed with relief and muttered, "All right!"

Sergeant Bill Perkins removed his helmet. "Whew! You guys okay?"

Lou moaned a bit—he was kidding. "I think I'm going to be sore tomorrow."

Officer Jim Dunlop got out his set of keys and unlocked all the handcuffs. Lou, Nancy, Elijah, and Elisha, wrists free, got to their feet.

"Good work," said Perkins. Then he called toward the pantry, "Did we get all that on tape?"

The pantry door swung open, and Officer Kyle Warner, video camera in hand, made an "okay" sign with his thumb and finger. "Great performance, guys."

Perkins spoke into his portable radio, "Okay, we have the Gomez location: 401 Taylor." He signed off and smiled. "Our friend Mr. Gomez is in for a visit, along with Morelli, Baylor, Dorning, and, uh . . ."

Officer Warner helped him out. "Steve Vernon. We needed a lead on that guy."

"And now we've got it!" Perkins extended his hand for a congratulatory shake. "Nate, Sarah, thanks a lot."

Nate and Sarah Springfield, who had been posing as "Lou" and "Nancy" for the past two months, shook his hand.

"But Nate," said Perkins, who really *was* from the East Coast, "the Philadelphia accent could use a little work."

"You'd know," Nate responded with a laugh, his own accent reflecting his Montana roots.

Perkins shook hands with Nate and Sarah's sixteen-year-old twins, Elijah and Elisha. "You okay?"

They were both breathing a lot easier and smiling for the first time, as if they didn't really want the whole world to drop dead after all.

"Oh, *we're* intact," said Elijah, gathering up the pieces of his shattered fake video camera. "I worked three days on this."

Elisha removed a black wig and shook loose her shoulder-length blond hair. "But what about Marv? What's going to happen to him?"

"We're making it look as much like a real drug bust as possible," Perkins said.

"You had *me* convinced," Nate said.

"Well, hopefully, word will get around that Marv's out for good, and that should keep the local gangs and drug dealers from trying to come after him. We have a family from one of the churches who is willing to take him in on a mentor program. It's a strict environment with plenty of rules, but that's why the prosecutor's willing to work with us. It works." Perkins smiled. "A strict environment with total accountability, but with the love of a family and the love of God."

"Has anyone been able to find Marv's real family?" Sarah asked.

"We'll need Marv to help us out on that one." Perkins wagged his head in dismay. "Sometimes runaways have a home to return to, and sometimes . . . well, we'll just have to see."

"It's just so hard to believe," said Nate. "How old *is* Marv, anyway?"

"He can't be more than fourteen," said Perkins. "Gomez finds them young, hungry, and alone."

"Well, he won't be hungry and alone anymore."

Perkins smiled. "Not if we can help it."

"So . . . ," Nate's eyes scanned the room. "Let's go, folks. We need to give this house back to the owners so they can get back to renting it. Gather up the gear—and whose cat is that?"

While Perkins and Dunlop discussed who might own the cat, the Springfields opened cupboards and drawers, removing dishes, silverware, groceries, and dishtowels they'd placed there to make the kitchen look lived in. They also removed microphones strategically hidden behind the window shades, the ceiling light fixture, and under the counter.

"Oh, by the way, Nate," said Sergeant Perkins, "Morgan called. He needs you to call him back right away."

"Thanks," Nate replied, stepping out onto the back porch and opening his cell phone. He punched in a number, the phone beeping with each entry.

A woman's voice answered after one ring. "*Veritas* Project."

"This is Nate Springfield."

"Ah, hello, Nate. Hang on, I'll connect you."

In only a few seconds, a man's voice came on the phone. "Nate. How'd it go?"

Nate looked toward the kitchen and the cleanup going on. "We have Marv."

"Wonderful!"

"He was the last drug slave working for Gomez, so that clears that out. And now we finally got the information we needed on Gomez and the others, so there goes the drug ring—hopefully."

"Excellent! And what do you think of their antidrug program?"

Nate smiled. "The reports we got were on the money. The police and prosecutors are joining up with the community and the churches too, and they're working the problem at a heart level. I guess they're finally starting to see that if you change the heart, the life will change with it. They've seen it work."

"Think it'll work for Marv?"

"Well . . ." Nate gave it some thought. "It worked for those other two kids Gomez owned. As for Marv, well, we've gotten to know him a while, and I think he has a good chance of turning things around. We've got a Christian family lined up to take him in. We'll just have to let God do the rest from there."

"So the Truth works."

Nate had to chuckle. "Well, yeah, if you give it a chance. The problem is, if you really want the Truth, then you have to have God along with it, and that gets a little sticky. If you can persuade the courts and communities to give God's ways a try, then yeah, the Truth works—and that's what I intend to report to the President."

"Good enough. Now get ready for another one. We just got

word of something brewing in Baker, Washington. Some kids are getting sick and demented, and no one knows why. Could be drugs, could be toxic contamination, could be a disease—or it could be something nobody's even thought of. Drug Enforcement's been called, and so have Environmental Protection and the Centers for Disease Control, but they're all backlogged and it's going to take them weeks to get on it. Nate, the President wants you in Baker now. There are . . . well, let's say there are certain undercurrents at that school, certain issues that the other agencies won't be looking for. The President is counting on you to get this thing solved before these other people have a chance to muddle it all up with politics and press releases. As always, Nate, for the record . . ."

"I know," Nate had heard this disclaimer so often he had it memorized. "The President wants to know the reasons, not just the facts. The *Veritas* Project has nothing to do with his administration. The job is strictly unofficial, strictly up to me if I want to take it."

"You've got it." Morgan laughed.

Nate took out his pen and pad. "Go ahead."

"We were contacted by a counselor named Tom Gessner from the high school. . . ."

☙❧

Shortly afterward, Nate read from his notes, sharing the potential new assignment with his family as they stood in the now-empty kitchen.

Sarah was intrigued. "There's definitely a spiritual aspect to it."

Elijah looked a little "iffy" about it. "Yeah, but I'll bet it means going to school again."

Elisha wrinkled her nose. "Another *school* case?"

"Ehh, so whatza matta?" Nate asked, his East Coast accent returning. "You got somethin' against school?"

"Oh, Dad, pull-eeezzz!"

2

THE GHOST AND
THE ANGEL

NATE SPRINGFIELD WAS tall but not imposing, strong but not brutish, the kind of man who could have played the part of a quiet but intense town marshal in an old western movie—he even wore the jeans, lamb-collared coat, and Stetson hat to convey the image. He loved his family and loved being home, and he counted it fortunate that, when the unusual work of The *Veritas* Project required a bit of traveling, the whole family traveled together. Yesterday, they had helped the police crack open a drug ring in Montague, Oregon—and examined whether or not the police and the community had an antidrug program that really worked. Today, he had an appointment with a competent but somewhat anxious high school counselor in the town of Baker, Washington—and exactly what The Project was about to encounter, he could only guess.

He was clean-shaven and recently showered—no more of the "Lou" image, at least for now—as he stepped out of his car and quietly surveyed the Baker High School campus, as old as Baker itself but recently rebuilt. What was once an old brick and lap-sided schoolhouse was now a modern structure with computerized classrooms, wide open hallways, a vast cafeteria and commons, covered walkways, hedges, planting beds, and a marvelous gym and athletic facility. Classes were in session, so the campus was quiet, with hardly a body visible except through some of the classroom windows. The place looked orderly and peaceful, just as most high schools in most small towns did.

Which raised the question: Did most high schools in most small towns have a metal detector just inside the front door? Nate had to remove his belt and car keys before the metal detector would let him through without beeping. It was a cruel reminder of a new reality in public schools. Parents all over town still trusted this to be a safe place for their kids to learn and challenge life. Unfortunately— and so hard to face!—this was also a place where bizarre and dangerous things were not *supposed* to happen, but *could*.

To hear Tom Gessner tell it, bizarre and dangerous things were happening all right—things the metal detectors were powerless to prevent.

Nate got his belt and keys back from the student attendant and entered the main hall, a long, echoing passage with poster-plastered bulletin boards announcing anything and everything in loud, eye-catching colors and a voluminous trophy case proudly displaying the glories and awards of many a winning team over the years. Down the hall in both directions were numbered classroom doors and lockers, lockers, lockers. Beyond that, the start of more halls, more posters, more lockers. A newcomer might get lost in here. The glassed-in school office was right across the hall from the main doors. He went inside, signed in, and got directions to Gessner's office.

ᐂ

"Nate Springfield!" Tom Gessner, a young man with close-cropped hair and beard, got up from his desk and offered his hand.

Nate shook his hand and admired Gessner's cozy little office. Gessner was new on the faculty this year, but it wasn't hard to see he was well qualified and experienced. The informal snapshots, funny little gifts from students, mementos from other jobs in other places—not to mention several degrees displayed on the walls—testified to that.

A uniformed police officer also rose and offered his hand. Gessner introduced him. "Nate Springfield, this is Dan Carrillo, in charge of security." Carrillo was a shorter man, a bit thin, and nervous, like a tight little terrier. He shook Nate's hand and muttered hello, but didn't appear too happy. Gessner continued, "He's an officer with the Baker police, and this year we have him on campus full time to handle security." Then he added with a twinkle in his eye, "He came with the metal detectors."

"And to serve as liaison between the school and the police department," Carrillo added boldly. "When you talk to me, you're talking to the Baker City Police—and they're talking to you." That last line came across as a stern reminder.

Nate noticed Officer Carrillo's badge, gun, belt radio, night stick, handcuffs, and beeper. He was serious about this. "It's a pleasure to meet you, sir," Nate said.

"Maybe." Officer Carrillo closed the office door as Gessner

gestured to an empty chair. "But let's be clear from the beginning. *Mr. Gessner's* the one who called you in—"

"My pastor had read about you," Gessner shared proudly.

Carrillo continued, irritated by the interruption. "But I'm still not convinced you're needed."

"Well, this would be a good time to find that out," Nate replied, looking in Gessner's direction.

Gessner sat in his desk chair and rotated it toward the center of the room, facing Carrillo and Nate. "Well, Mr. Springfield comes with some impressive references from police departments all over the country." He handed Carrillo a folder crammed with pages of information. "Take a look. He and his associates—his wife and kids, to be exact—have done undercover work, crime-scene reconstruction, sting operations, you name it."

Carrillo scanned the papers and scowled. "The *Veritas* Project? What's that?"

"It's what we are and what we do," said Nate. "We're privately funded—"

"Which means they don't cost us a cent!" Gessner inserted.

"—to investigate unusual cases and uncover the Truth, whatever it is."

Carrillo read further. "'Judeo-Christian principles applied to case study.' . . . Is this religious?"

Nate chuckled. "No. We just employ a tried-and-true way of looking at things."

"And considering what we're up against," said Gessner, "their way of looking at things could be exactly what we need."

"A way of *looking* at things?" Carrillo asked, his skepticism obvious.

"Our country's having its problems, Officer Carrillo," Nate explained. "We've got drugs, disease, crime, violence, the breakup of the home, and that's just naming a few. Now, everybody likes to find something or someone to blame, but we're saying a big part of the reason is that we've lost sight of God. When you lose sight of God, you lose sight of what the Truth is. When The *Veritas* Project investigates a case, we assume up front that the Truth is the Truth, even if it isn't popular, even if we don't like it. The Truth is like God: It is what it is, and you can't change it, and you can't ignore it."

Carrillo nodded to himself. "A philosopher!" He scolded Gessner, "You bring us a philosopher when what we really need is more cops!" He looked at Nate. "No offense, Mr. Springfield, but I don't see what all this, this touchy-feely, get-to-the-heart stuff has to do with our problem here."

"I think it has everything to do with it," Gessner countered. "But you don't have to worry about Mr. Springfield's qualifications. Both he and his wife, Sarah, were with the FBI for several years; he was a county sheriff, and she was a professor of criminology and forensics at the University of Washington. Because they're independent and privately funded, they can do the kind of investigating the police don't have the time or the budget to do."

Carrillo turned to Nate. "So just what are you going to do that the police and the health department *and* the medical pros haven't already done? We've checked all the locker rooms, the kitchen, the food in the cafeteria, the candy in the candy machines, the pop in the pop machines, the water, everything. We've interviewed all kinds of kids who had any contact with the victims. We've done background checks and looked for illegal drugs."

"We'll just take it from there," Nate answered, "just build on what you've started and see what we find."

☙❧

Out on the sidewalk that circled the school, two students wearing yellow grounds-crew badges around their necks pushed a trash can on a cart and looked for litter.

Elijah pushed the cart and watched as a meter attached to the cartwheels ticked off the school building's dimensions. "One hundred forty, one hundred forty-five . . ."

Elisha carried a pointed stick and jabbed at litter wherever she found it—even as she verified the number of classrooms along this side of the building. "Four rooms . . . this one's a cloakroom and storage . . . and that should be the girls' rest room. The windows have swing latches, no cranks."

☙❧

Nate pulled a small writing pad from his shirt pocket and leafed through some notes he'd taken. "Now, when Mr. Gessner and I talked on the phone, he told me you've had three kids get sick so far . . . Tod Kramer, a junior; Doug Anderson, a senior; and now there's Jim Boltz, a senior—and all of them are athletes."

"We checked those three real close," Carrillo answered. "None of them had any record of drug abuse. We even considered whether this might be some kind of sabotage of our football team, some kind of hallucinogenic drug slipped into their food or drinks by an opposing school. Baker was hot this year. They were headed for the state championship."

"But so far, no evidence of sabotage?"

"No. The doctors at the hospital haven't found a thing."

Gessner offered, "We've pretty much ruled out any kind of disease or contagion. After all, hundreds of students use the same gym facilities every day, but we've only had three cases of"—he looked at Carrillo—"Abel Frye syndrome."

Carrillo only sneered.

Nate eyed them curiously. *"Abel Frye syndrome?"*

Carrillo shot a glance at Gessner before answering Nate. "Mr. Gessner hasn't told you about the symptoms?"

Nate could recall them. "Loss of coordination and muscle strength, severe paranoia, hallucinations, unconsciousness."

Gessner added, "All three athletes are still hospitalized, drifting in and out of consciousness. And when they are conscious— they're out of their minds."

"So crazy they have to be tied to their beds," said Carrillo, "and talking gibberish—except for muttering 'Abel Frye' every once in a while." He sniffed in disgust. " 'Abel Frye.' It's crazy."

Nate asked, "Is that a name?"

Gessner nodded. "There's a legend here at Baker—"

Carrillo moaned and folded his arms. "Oh, boy, here we go!"

Gessner paused to gather himself. Apparently, what he was about to say wasn't going to be easy. "It's why I wanted to find outside help, a third party who would understand. Around here, you don't talk about this stuff without jeopardizing your job, your reputation . . ."

Carrillo chuckled and rolled his eyes.

Gessner pushed on, "You see, I have some thoughts, some suspicions that move into a realm the police—and the school board, and the principal, I might add—are presently unwilling to explore. I can't be sure of anything at this point. We need more data—"

"Gessner, would you just spit it out?" Carrillo barked.

"Mr. Springfield, we have a ghost."

ତଡ଼ତ

Casually, quietly, Sarah Springfield strolled down the hallways of Baker High, pointing her digital camera and snapping pictures of doorways, corners, rows of lockers, windows, display cases, exit doors, stairways. She'd almost finished her first walk-through of the school's halls and planned two more before leaving.

After a quick look in both directions, she stepped up to a locker, rested her cheek against the metal door, and gently began turning the knob of the combination lock. Right . . . stop. Left . . . stop. Right . . . right a little more . . .

Click. The locker opened and she examined the inner structure. Okay. Typical.

∽

Tom Gessner pulled a rolled-up piece of paper off a shelf. "It's a *belief,* a *legend,* right? Like a school mascot." He unrolled the paper and displayed a strange painted portrait. "This was painted by a student for last month's art contest. Meet Abel Frye."

The painting showed a gruesome specter, a young man, or maybe a boy, clearly dead and decaying, the head cocked grotesquely against the right shoulder as if the neck were broken, the black, sunken eyes staring with both terror and menace. He wore a shredded, tattered shirt, a golden-eyed hawk sat on his shoulder, and one bony hand was extended as if the thing wanted to reach out from the painting and grab a victim.

"This painting won first prize," Gessner explained. "The artist is a girl named Crystal Sparks. She's one of the students out on the fringe, so to speak, quite possibly involved in witchcraft. This painting was posted on the bulletin board in the main hall for two weeks, and now there are photocopies floating around. Thanks to this painting, we have universal agreement around the school as to what Abel Frye looks like."

"And just who is he supposed to be?" Nate asked.

"According to the legend, this is the ghost of a young man, a student, who hanged himself in the stairwell of the old building clear back in the 1930s." He pulled a small map from a drawer, a

38

layout of the present building. "Our present school building was built in place of the old one six years ago, and part of the building is sitting where the old building used to be."

"The kids have it all figured out," said Carrillo. "The ghost is still haunting the area where the kid hanged himself."

Gessner traced it out on the map. "This rearmost hallway, to be exact, running right alongside the gym. The stairwell of the old building used to be right there."

Carrillo mockingly widened his eyes and acted spooky as he said, "They call it the *Forbidden Hallway!*"

Gessner admitted, "The more superstitious kids won't go near that hallway, and since these weird outbreaks, six students have asked for new locker assignments. The point is, for many students at this school, our ghost is more than just a spooky little legend—and he's getting more 'real' all the time. The name cropped up only recently."

"So was there ever a real Abel Frye?"

Carrillo shrugged.

Gessner shook his head. "There's no record of an Abel Frye ever attending this school."

Nate exhaled thoughtfully, still staring at the painting. "Okay. Keep going."

"They call it the Forbidden Hallway!"

Elijah and Elisha walked a wide circle around the school grounds, getting familiar with the fences and shrubs that bordered two sides and the line of forest that bordered the rear.

"It's not a hard school to sneak up on," Elisha noted.

"Or to sneak away from," Elijah added. He was holding a site plan of the school and grounds. He studied it again, comparing it to what they were seeing. "Dad was right. The building looks a little cockeyed, like somebody forgot something somewhere."

"Sightings of the ghost have become more frequent," Tom Gessner continued. "Several students claim to have seen him, or smelled him, or heard him. We even have some who believe—unless they're just pretending—that the ghost can bless or curse the football games, so they bring him offerings of candy or cookies the day of each game to make sure we'll win."

"Guess they offered the wrong cookies," said Carrillo. "The three victims were star players on the team."

That was supposed to be funny, but Gessner didn't laugh. "It might be something like that."

"*What?*"

"Listen to this." He looked toward the door, apparently to make sure it was closed and they were talking in private. He actually lowered his voice as he told them, "I spoke with three students just days ago—two girls, both juniors, and one boy, a senior. They were here in the building for an evening play rehearsal—we're doing *The Crucible* this year—and they got adventurous. During part of the play when they weren't required onstage, they sneaked off to that back hallway. It was a dare. They were probably trying to scare each other."

Nate nodded. "Sure."

"All three heard a voice in that hallway, coming from nowhere, coming from *everywhere,* and it was speaking a name over and over—the name of our fallen quarterback, Jim Boltz."

"It's a prank," said Carrillo. "*Sure* they're going to hear Jim Boltz's name. Jim Boltz went nuts hollering the name of the ghost. Everybody in the school knows that."

Gessner shot back, "They came to see me the Wednesday *before* the game in which Jim Boltz was stricken."

Nate leaned back, his fingers stroking his face. Carrillo was notably silent.

Gessner continued, "I know these kids and, sure, they can be silly and impressionable at times, but this time they were sincere, and they were frightened. They heard something and they all corroborate each other." He looked at Carrillo. "And I'm sure you'll agree, Jim Boltz being in the hospital is no prank."

There was silence in the room. Finally, Carrillo muttered, "This is getting creepy."

Sarah strolled through the empty lunchroom, taking note of the food vending machines and the number and kinds of goodies being offered. She poked her head out through the one exit door to see where it went then stepped back from the door, watching to see if it would swing closed and latch by itself. It did. She went into the kitchen, showed her visitor pass to the ladies working there, and started having a friendly chat.

⟨✺⟩

"Have the three victims offended anybody?" Nate asked. "Do they have enemies?"

Gessner was visibly impressed. "Ah. You know where I'm going." He stood. "Gentlemen, I have something to show you— and please, let's not discuss this where we can be heard."

They followed Tom Gessner through the office compound and resource library, down the main hall, and from there down another hall to the far end of the building. They passed by the gym and could hear the sounds of a P.E. class—echoed shouts, the pounding of a basketball, the squeaking of tennis shoes—coming from inside. Going past the gym, they rounded a corner and stopped.

"The Forbidden Hallway," Gessner said in a near whisper.

It ran the length of the gym. One wall was a common wall with the gym, lined with lockers. The other was an exterior wall with windows and exit doors. Plenty of light came through the windows and light fixtures in the ceiling. There was absolutely nothing spooky about it.

Gessner walked down that hall, and Nate and Carrillo followed. Halfway down the hall, he stopped at a particular locker.

"Jim Boltz's locker," he said.

"Thoroughly searched by myself and the health department," Carrillo reminded them.

"But did anyone notice this?" Gessner pointed to a small scratch mark in the upper right corner of the door.

They examined it closely. Nate put on a pair of glasses for an even closer look.

"What about it?" Carrillo asked.

"A hanging man," said Nate.

"Exactly," said Gessner.

Carrillo had to take a second look. "Well, I'll be."

"I checked the lockers of the other two victims, Tod Kramer and Doug Anderson. They have the same mark, a tiny hanging figure scratched in the paint. The connection with Abel Frye is obvious."

"I checked the lockers of the other two victims, Tod Kramer and Doug Anderson. They have the same mark, a tiny hanging figure scratched in the paint. The connection with Abel Frye is obvious."

"So," said Nate, "whether it's a ghost or not, somebody's up to something."

"Could be a sick prank," said Carrillo. "Something done after the victims were hit."

"Of course," said Gessner. "But you'll notice the five-pointed shape, as if derived from a pentagram, a symbol used in witchcraft. These days, witchcraft and satanism among high school students are not uncommon, and from what I hear from the students, they could be happening here."

"Are you saying the victims were *hexed?*"

"I'm saying that a certain group could exist in this school that would wish them harm."

Carrillo smirked. "Eh, as long as they're not packing guns I'm not too worried."

"*I* worry about what would make them want to harm others in the first place." Gessner gestured at the strange symbol. "Kids usually get into witchcraft for the same reasons: the desire for power, the need for self-esteem and to be a part of something, the need to have some kind of control over their lives, especially when life treats them cruelly—" Then he added, "—when *other kids* treat them cruelly."

Carrillo cocked an eyebrow. "So you think these jocks were picking on somebody?"

Gessner looked at them both, a sadness in his eyes. "Kids can be terribly cruel to each other. We don't know the half of it. We don't always see it. The kids don't report it." Then he added with a touch of anger in his eyes, "And all too often the teachers allow it—and some even encourage it."

"So now somebody's trying to get even."

Gessner spread his empty hands. "From here on out, gentlemen, we have nothing but unknowns."

"So let's just round up these witches and start asking some questions," Carrillo said.

"We don't know who they are," Gessner said.

"Come on, you see the kids every day!"

"Not all of them. That's simply not possible."

Carrillo was careful to keep his voice down. "How about Ian Snyder? That kid put a straight pin through his tongue right in front of a teacher and then asked her what she'd do if he ever pulled a gun on her. He's been suspended a couple of times."

"Do you honestly think he'd tell you anything?" Gessner asked.

Carrillo didn't have an answer for that. They all knew it was highly unlikely.

"And for every Ian Snyder there are at least ten wallpaper kids."

"Uh, excuse me," said Nate. "*Wallpaper* kids?"

"The kids who just blend in. They never say anything, never call attention to themselves, never cause trouble, certainly never talk to their high school counselor, and that's the problem. We don't know what they might be feeling and thinking, or what they might be capable of. Having a school full of wallpaper kids can be more scary than having a few Ian Snyders around."

Carrillo had to chew on that for a long moment. "So we don't know who these witches are."

"No," Gessner answered. "After all, just what is a witch supposed to look like?"

"Well, who have the jocks been picking on?"

"We have to find out."

Carrillo was getting impatient. "Well, we sure don't know a whole lot, do we?"

"Only that three athletes are in the hospital under very strange circumstances and we need to know *something*." Gessner looked at Nate. "And that's where you come in, Mr. Springfield. We need you and your family to fill in all these blanks. We need you to be here and blend in, to see and hear things, to get a feel for what might be happening—from your unique perspective."

Nate took one more look at the sinister symbol on the locker, thought for a moment, then replied, "We can start tomorrow—if that's okay with Officer Carrillo."

Carrillo asked, "Well, just what do you intend to do?"

Nate smiled. "Blend in, I suppose. Just be ourselves. I'll go on staff, my kids will enroll as students, my wife will do research in the background."

They started back toward Gessner's office.

"Okay," said Carrillo, "I'll go along with it as long as you understand you're answering to me—and Ms. Wyrthen, the principal."

"Sounds fine to me."

"Ms. Wyrthen's all right. She's all business, but she's got a good heart for the kids. You should get along all right."

෨෪

Sarah, Elijah, and Elisha met Nate the moment he came out the front door.

"We're on the case," he told them as they walked toward their car. "Got the site layout?"

Elijah held up the site plan, now marked and modified with a red pen. "You were right. The building and grounds don't line up with the plan the county has on file."

"The woods are closer than the plans show, and there are lots of hiding places," Elisha pointed out.

"The security's pretty good, though," said Sarah. "The doors and windows are sound, with good locks and good alarms."

"Anybody get a student roster?" Nate asked.

"Got that from the office, along with all the class schedules. It's a lot of material to go through."

"Well, let's do the easy stuff first. And let's get Mr. Maxwell going. There should be *something* to smell around here."

"So when do we have to enroll?" Elijah asked, actually cringing.

"You're enrolled now," Nate said with a smile. "Mr. Gessner and I took care of it. You start tomorrow."

෨෪

An ominous sign was posted outside the door to the hospital ward: QUARANTINE AREA: AUTHORIZED PERSONNEL ONLY.

Two mothers and one father were just coming out of the room. All three were in tears.

Since the school district and the local police had authorized them, the Springfields were admitted, but only when accompanied by the physician in charge, and only after donning hospital masks and gowns. They walked in slowly, taking in the details and trying to understand the horror of what they were seeing. It was a clean and sterile hospital room, and yet they couldn't shake the feeling that they'd entered a compartment in hell, a prison for tortured souls filled with garbled sounds, sickening smells, frightening visions.

There were four beds in the room. Three were occupied.

Dr. Stuart, a gentle, gray-haired man, spoke through his surgical mask as he stopped at the first bed. "This is Tod Kramer."

Tod was once a handsome, red-haired youth, but not now. He lay there motionless, his eyes staring vacantly at the ceiling, his skin like thin yellow parchment, his hands limp and withering. They could see his lips silently stuttering under the clear plastic oxygen mask.

"He's been here twelve days," Dr. Stuart said.

In the next bed lay a large-framed African-American youth. He was staring vacantly as well, but his eyes were moving slightly as if seeing frightening visions, and his fingers twitched and trembled. He was muttering nonstop, but there were no understandable words. There was an IV in his arm and there were feeding tubes in his nose, but he was breathing without an oxygen mask.

"This is Doug Anderson. He's been here seven days."

They turned and faced the bed opposite Doug's. They'd already seen news photos and Jim Boltz's senior picture, but they never could have anticipated the crazed creature they now saw before them. He was tied to the bed at both his wrists and ankles. He had needles in both arms and tubes up his nose. His eyes were wide with fright and constantly rolling as if watching demons flutter just above the bed. His head kept jerking and twitching, his fingers blindly groping, and he was whimpering in the language of madness: ". . . over in wainswen badooly gone thump . . . mater raining dig the fleenincrab . . ."

Sarah looked from Jim to Doug to Tod. "It's degenerative."

Dr. Stuart nodded grimly. "It worsens steadily from day to day. If we can't reverse it, in ten days, Jim will be in the same condition as Tod."

"And Tod?"

Dr. Stuart shook his head. "We may not be able to keep him alive. He needs oxygen now. Before long he'll need a full respirator. After that . . ."

Elisha leaned over the foot of Jim Boltz's bed, listening intently, watching Jim's face. "What's he saying?"

Dr. Stuart shook his head. "It's gibberish. Aimless ravings. The boys aren't communicative. We can't talk to them; they can't talk to us."

Elijah asked, "Has he ever mentioned the name Abel Frye?"

Jim Boltz stiffened and gasped as if shocked with electricity, so suddenly it made them all jump. The rambling gibberish stopped. Jim lay there, eyes locked on one spot above him, his jaw quivering. A weak, trembling sound crossed his lips. ". . . Abel . . . Frye . . ."

Dr. Stuart hurried to the bedside. "He's never done this before."

Nate hurried to the other side of the bed and took a small digital recorder from his carry bag. "If it's okay with you?"

Dr. Stuart nodded.

Nate pressed the record button and held the recorder close to Jim's mouth.

The steady "beep" from the heart monitor beside the bed accelerated as Jim's pulse raced. He no longer muttered but spoke, so softly they all bent close to hear him. "Abel Frye . . . Abel Frye . . ."

Dr. Stuart waved a finger in front of Jim's eyes. The eyes didn't follow it but remained locked where they were, on some invisible, terrible image.

"The angel . . . ," said Jim, tugging at his restraints. "The angel . . . the angel and Abel Frye. No, no, don't look at me . . ."

"Jim?" the doctor prompted.

"He's coming . . . he's coming . . ."

"Who, Jim?"

"The angel . . . the angel and Abel Frye."

"The angel?"

Jim's head relaxed. The heart monitor began to slow down. "Barsinolla baker team on the boromoommmm . . ."

Dr. Stuart straightened, frustration visible all over his face.

Nate let the recorder run on, recording a minute or two of Jim's mutterings. As far as anyone could tell, Jim said nothing else intelligible.

They huddled in the middle of the room, speaking in low tones.

"Who is Abel Frye?" asked Dr. Stuart.

"The school ghost," said Nate.

He looked at them with the shocked and unbelieving expression one might expect. "A ghost and an angel?"

"Well," said Sarah, "it isn't much, but it's a start."

Dr. Stuart looked at the Springfields and then nodded with grim understanding. "Please hurry. Time is of the essence, if we hope to save their lives."

3

THE LEGEND OF ABEL FRYE

THE BELL RANG, the classroom doors burst open, and the hallways of Baker High School filled for another five-minute rush between classes. Nine hundred kids, all shapes, all sizes, scampered, lumbered, strode, marched, or just plain walked with books in arms, packs on backs, clothing in a zillion different colors, and everything in the world to say to each other before the bell rang again.

In the main hall, a janitor in gray coveralls stayed close to the wall to keep from being trampled, and as he worked, he watched, studying their faces, their expressions. He counted quickly, wondering how many young people would pass by that one spot in five minutes. When he held still and kept his eyes aimed straight across the hall, he could almost sense that *he* was moving.

The only other body not moving was Officer Carrillo. He was standing just outside the school office with the steadiness of a courthouse pillar and the authoritative air of a traffic light, his arms folded across his chest, his beady eyes following the flow. As far as anyone knew, he'd never pulled his gun or used his night stick, but he still carried them—and you just couldn't help being impressed.

The five minutes shrank to three and the number of migrating bodies dwindled. Two new faces passed by, a boy and a girl. They looked so much alike they had to be brother and sister, maybe even twins. The boy had a calculus text under his arm and the girl was carrying the script from *The Crucible*. Bright kids.

Two minutes and it was almost quiet.

One minute, and the last kids left in the halls were looking worried and walking as fast as they could without running.

The bell rang. Up and down the halls, the last echoes of footsteps faded, the big classroom doors closed with a metallic clunk.

And now the halls were empty.

Carrillo looked left and right, then sauntered across the hall to where the janitor stood. "Hey, Springfield. Those two new kids . . . they yours?"

Nate Springfield didn't look up, but proceeded to reline a trash can as he replied, "I cannot tell a lie. Yes, they are. I've started work here as a janitor, and they've enrolled as students— but we aren't going to call attention to this, are we?"

"Sorry."

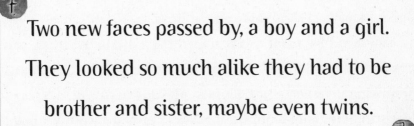

Two new faces passed by, a boy and a girl. They looked so much alike they had to be brother and sister, maybe even twins.

The door to the office swung open with the low, heavy note of its big hinges, and they heard a quick, staccato sound like a judge's gavel coming toward them—*pock, pock, pock*—high heels on tile.

"Here comes Ms. Wyrthen," said Carrillo.

Ms. Wyrthen, the high school principal, dressed in gray and looking grim, came at them like a queen in a hurry. "The halls should remain clear until lunch period. We're ready when you are."

Nate crossed to the front door and pushed it open so a smiling, panting golden retriever could come in, pulling along a well-dressed businesswoman at the other end of his leash. Nate introduced the woman. "Ms. Wyrthen, I'd like to introduce my wife, Sarah."

Ms. Wyrthen's eyebrows went up as she extended her hand. "Charmed, I'm sure."

Nate lovingly roughed up the dog's ears. "And this is Mr. Maxwell. We call him Max."

Ms. Wyrthen smiled and gave a slight nod. "Mr. Loman is waiting for us."

Ms. Wyrthen, Nate, Sarah, Mr. Maxwell, and Officer Carrillo started down the hall, Ms. Wyrthen's heels *pock-pocking* and Mr. Maxwell's nails *click-clicking* on the floor.

Nate was just about to say something, but Ms. Wyrthen said it first. "Officer Carrillo, it may look a little obvious, four of us all walking together, especially with the dog . . ."

He took the hint—not happily—and turned away after other business.

Sarah handed Mr. Maxwell's leash to Nate. "And if you could show me the way to the library . . ."

Ms. Wyrthen pointed. "Up those stairs, second floor, to the right. Mrs. Aimsley is expecting you."

Sarah gave Nate a special smile, then headed for the stairs.

Now it was just Nate, Mr. Maxwell, and Ms. Wyrthen.

Ms. Wyrthen spoke softly. "Thank you for being here, Mr. Springfield. I hope you understand that our arrangement with you is tenuous at best, and time is in very short supply. Some of the parents are getting frightened and want to close the school down; others are getting angry and want the school kept open—they don't want us to forfeit our bid for the state football championship. The school board is up in arms. They voted to spend precious district funds on the metal detectors and a security officer, but now the school still isn't safe and they're looking foolish. I'm willing to try anything to protect our kids, but now the parents are pressuring me from opposite extremes and the school board is telling me they don't want to give this problem too *much* attention."

Nate was genuinely troubled. "I promise we'll do all we can, as quickly as we can, and if we find out our services aren't needed, we'll be out of here before our shadows can catch up."

She sighed and wagged her head. "This is supposed to be a safe school environment. There are no guns here, no knives, no dangerous weapons of any kind. We have a full-time security officer, the first in the school district. We're the first school in the district to install a metal detector. We've prided ourselves on our ability to maintain order and discipline." She looked at him. "But trouble still gets through the doors."

They rounded a corner and met a bespectacled, balding fellow wearing gray coveralls similar to Nate's and a sizable key ring on his belt. His kind, smiling face was certainly a pleasant contrast to Ms. Wyrthen's. "Well, hello there, Mr. Springfield. How are the wastebaskets?"

"Finished up the main hall," said Nate, "but that one near the lunchroom is going to need a couple extra bags."

Mr. Loman laughed. "Okay, well done!" Then he scratched Mr. Maxwell's ears. "So this is Mr. Maxwell!" Mr. Maxwell leaned into Mr. Loman's scratches, a happy, dazed look on his face. "How about it, Maxie? You want to be a janitor, too?"

Ms. Wyrthen was getting impatient. "Mr. Springfield would like his dog to smell the three victims' lockers."

"Let's go," said Mr. Loman, leading the way, his key ring jangling with each step. "Of course, you know, the police already had their dog in here sniffing for drugs. They didn't find anything."

"Well, still I'd like to bring Max up to speed," said Nate. "We might need his services later on."

Mr. Loman led them to a row of lockers not far from the gym and paused by locker number 392. "This is Tod Kramer's locker."

Nate examined the locker door. The mysterious symbol of a hanging man was etched in the upper right corner, just as Gessner reported. Nate called no attention to the symbol, but tapped the locker to show Max which one to sniff. Max sniffed, but didn't react.

"Well, we took everything out of it," Mr. Loman explained, glancing at a tattered notebook for the combination and spinning the dial. "All the contents of the lockers in question are being stored in Officer Carrillo's office."

He turned the latch and opened the door.

Max stuck his head in the locker and sniffed the corners and everywhere his head would reach. He seemed bored.

Nate was satisfied. "Okay, let's move on."

They headed down the hall. Two more lockers to go.

ↂ

Second lunch period. The lunchroom was full of students with sack lunches, vending-machine snacks, soft drinks, salads, and sweets. Music was playing over a sound system. Lockers up and down the halls were banging. Kids were talking loudly to each other so they could hear each other over all the kids talking loudly to each other.

At first glance, they were one big, noisy crowd, but at second glance, this crowd had its subgroups, its tribes. At the center row of tables, the athletic ones were bragging and jabbing about sports, any sports, who was good and who was better; a few rows over, the math and science geeks hunched and huddled over their equations and pocket computers; on the far side, the artistic types talked about drama, *The Crucible,* a video project; against a row of lockers, a bunch of rowdy males performed their daily ritual of leaning against the cold metal and looking down their noses for weaker kids to pick on; and on a bench along the wall, a clump of dark-clothed, bizarre-looking outcasts glowered and formed a group by being different from everyone except each other.

Elijah Springfield, no longer posing as a dope-peddling misfit from Montague, Oregon, had found acceptance among the math and science bunch. He was a handsome, sandy-haired young man of average height and wiry build, his soft hazel eyes framed behind wire-rimmed glasses. He was not especially outgoing, but his smile was warm and welcoming, and he'd managed to find something in common with two megabrains from calculus class, skinny Carl and pimply-faced Trevor. Right now, Trevor was trying to show Elijah the ropes in calculus.

"Okay," said Trevor, scribbling on a piece of paper as he spoke, "to differentiate this function, just use the Quotient Rule. In this case we would have x plus 1 times the derivative of x times x plus 3 . . ."

"Which is the derivative of x squared plus $3x$, which is $2x$ plus 3," said Carl.

"Brilliant, as always," Trevor quipped.

"Thank you."

Elijah listened intently, watching Carl and Trevor make their point.

"Subtract the numerator times the derivative of the denominator. . . ." Trevor continued, still scribbling, "x squared plus $3x$ times the derivative of x plus 1, and then divide the whole . . ."

Trevor stopped. He looked a little blank.

"Didn't work," said Carl.

Elijah scanned Trevor's calculations. "Umm . . . don't you have to square the denominator?"

Trevor scowled. "Where do you get that?"

"Well," said Elijah, taking his own pencil and scribbling on the same piece of paper, "it's the way the original integration formula works out: In the denominator you get the limit of v of x as h approaches zero, times the limit of v of x plus h as h approaches zero, and bingo, it's the same as v of x squared. Am I right?"

Trevor looked it over and broke into a grin. "Brilliant!"

"Above adequate!" said Carl.

"Thank you," said Elijah.

ೞ

Elisha Springfield was fitting in very nicely. She was naturally outgoing, had a gift for being comfortable around new people, and her attractiveness—there was no need to disguise it—had already turned some heads in the halls. By lunchtime, she'd made several new friends, both male and female—all had learned to pronounce her name E-*lee*-sha and not E-*lie*-sha—and right now she was sitting with two girls she'd met in drama class, chatty Karine and philosopher Sondra.

"I think Tituba's the heroine of the play," Karine was saying. "I mean, Arthur Miller was trying to point out the evils of religion and, I mean, isn't there a Tituba in all of us? We all want to be free to believe whatever we want without being judged for it."

"Well, of course. *The Crucible* is a cry for tolerance," Sondra agreed. "It's wrong for anyone to impose their morals on others. Very simple." Then she noticed Elisha smiling as if something was funny. "What?"

"You just said that something is wrong," Elisha replied, still smiling.

Sondra didn't get it. "So?"

Elisha explained, "You can't say it's wrong to impose your morals on others because, when you tell us something is wrong, you're imposing your morals on us, and you can't do that because you just said it's wrong to do that."

"Whooaa!" said Karine.

"Well, you know what I meant!" Sondra countered.

"Sure, but you see the problem? If the message of *The Crucible* is that everybody can believe whatever they want, and nobody's right and nobody's wrong, then why does the play disturb us? Where'd we ever get the idea that Tituba and John Proctor are the good guys and the Puritans are the bad guys? What makes us think that an injustice has been done or that there's anything right or wrong about *anything* in the play if there's no right or wrong?"

Sondra stopped to ponder that.

"That boy's looking at you!" Karine tittered. Elisha and Sondra started to look. "Don't look!" They didn't look.

"You mean Ian Snyder?" Sondra whispered.

Karine made a disgusted face. "*Eeugh*, don't make me sick!" She tried to point. "It's that other guy, that stud with the red hair . . ."

"Who's Ian Snyder?" Elisha asked.

"You don't want to meet him," said Karine. "He's really out there somewhere. I think he's a witch!"

"Just like the Tituba in all of us," Sondra observed.

"Huh?"

"Oh, nothing." For Elisha's benefit, she deftly pointed him out with her eyes and a barely discernible point of her finger. "Over there, by himself."

Elisha looked just long enough to see a thin, bizarre-looking kid sitting alone at the end of a row of tables. He seemed obsessed with the color black. He was dressed in black, had black hair—almost too black, as if he'd dyed it that way—and . . . had he even used something to blacken his lips and eyebrows? "He's a *witch*?"

Karine and Sondra made quick, downward motions with their hands. "Shhh."

"Time to tell her," Sondra said to Karine, and Karine nodded.

Elisha waited.

"You should know, there are weird things happening around here," Karine began.

"Ready to hear about our ghost?" Sondra asked, and she was serious.

⊙⃝⊙

"Oh, it's not news to me," said petite, gray-haired Mrs. Aimsley, bringing another stack of high school annuals to the table and setting them down with a thud. "We've had a ghost in this high school for as long as I can remember."

Sarah had set up her own little research center in a corner of the school library, one study table now burdened under stacks of yearbooks and enrollment records. Mrs. Aimsley turned out to be a very good source of information on the school and its traditions. She'd been the Baker High School librarian for the past forty years and had seen and heard just about everything. "So how did the legend start? Is there a true story behind it all?"

"*True* story?" Mrs. Aimsley had to laugh. "Well, which *true* story would you like to hear? There have been several."

"The one about Abel Frye," Sarah said.

❧

"He went to this school back in the 1930s," Karine explained, intrigued by her own tale. "And one night he hanged himself in the old school building."

Sondra added, "He lost his true love and decided to end it all."

❧

"Abel Frye. That name is new this year," said Mrs. Aimsley. She pulled one high school yearbook from the bottom of a stack and began to page through it. "There *was* a young man who hanged himself in the old school building, but his name wasn't Abel Frye."

She kept flipping pages as she tried to remember. "Lawrence . . . Macon? Masters? Matthews? I think it was the Class of 1933."

∞

Sondra had a photocopy of the Crystal Sparks painting in her notebook. She brought it out and showed Elisha. "Wholesome-looking character, isn't he?"

"So, was he a real person or is he just made up?"

"He was real, but the whole story's been covered up," Karine said in a hushed voice.

"It was such a terrible public relations nightmare that the school board destroyed all the records," Sondra explained. "They reprinted the high school yearbook and took Abel Frye's name out of it."

"And then there was a fire," Karine added with a spooky tone. "All the yearbooks with Abel Frye in them just happened to be burned in that fire."

Sondra was startled to hear that. "Since when?"

"You haven't heard about that?"

∞

Mrs. Aimsley found what she was looking for. "All right, here he is. Lawrence Matthews." She handed the yearbook to Sarah and pointed out the picture of a gaunt, homely kid with squinty eyes and oversized ears. "He was a farmer's son, I understand, and the Great Depression had left his family nearly destitute."

⊘⊘

"He was rich," said Sondra. "His family owned half the town back then."

"And he had a pet hawk that would sit on his shoulder," said Karine, "and he could sic it on other kids who tried to pick on him."

"They say he still has that hawk on his shoulder—well, the *ghost* does."

⊘⊘

"Lawrence never had a pet hawk that I know of, but he did raise chickens," said Mrs. Aimsley.

⊘⊘

Karine was talking faster and faster, the more excited she got. "He had a crush on a girl, but she fell for Abel's worst enemy, a jock, you know, the captain of the football team. Abel Frye was an underclassman, a little shrimpy guy, and all the jocks and upperclassmen picked on him—you know how it is. Anyway, all that and then losing the girl finally drove him over the edge. He lured the girl into the back stairway and stabbed her to death, and then he hanged himself from the old stairway railing."

॰ॐ॰

"The popular belief is that Lawrence's girlfriend was Mabel Johnson." Mrs. Aimsley pointed her out in the yearbook. "But she wasn't murdered; she died of influenza. Lawrence may have done away with himself out of grief, but . . ." She reflected a moment. "I think he had other problems in his life. He was homely, gaunt, from a very poor family. I can just imagine what kind of treatment he got from the other kids who had better clothes, shoes to wear, better abilities." She sighed and placed her hand mournfully on the page with Lawrence Matthews' picture. "I've seen many Lawrences come through this school, Mrs. Springfield, and sometimes I've wondered how they ever survived when all the other kids worked so hard to convince them they couldn't—or even *shouldn't*."

"He lured the girl into the back stairway and stabbed her to death, and then he hanged himself from the old stairway railing."

༄

In Officer Carrillo's office, Mr. Maxwell wasn't "alerting" as if finding any drugs, but he was certainly interested in *something* as he sniffed and sniffed at the contents of Doug Anderson's locker, now spread out on the floor. Nate and Carrillo were sitting at two sides of Carrillo's desk, watching and curious.

"What is it, Max?" Nate asked, knowing he wouldn't get a spoken answer.

Carrillo cracked, "Anderson's dirty socks, I'll bet. I think that's all you're going to find, the same kind of stuff we took from Tod Kramer's locker: textbooks, dirty socks, gym shoes, athletic gear, a few pin-up posters."

Nate wasn't so sure. "Well, if I know Max, I'd say he's on to something."

"But if it isn't drugs, what is it?"

"Beats me. Okay, Max, that'll do for now. Go lie down."

Max obeyed, flopping down in a corner of the room.

Wearing surgical gloves to prevent contamination of evidence, Nate reached down and pulled a muddy jersey from Doug Anderson's duffel bag. He examined it front and back. He set it aside. Then he pulled out Anderson's football shoes, looked inside them with a small penlight, examined the outside of each shoe, and put them aside. He checked the pants, the socks, a sweatshirt, and a tee shirt. Under all the clothing he found a tattered binder containing diagrams of football plays, some phone numbers of friends male and female, and some notes from a history class.

"I've got a question," he said.

"Yeah?"

"Did every member of the team have a duffel bag like this?"

"Sure. Standard issue."

Nate furrowed his brow. "We found Tod Kramer's and Doug Anderson's. Where's Jim Boltz's?"

Carrillo shrugged. "Hasn't turned up. We checked his home and his car, but zip. All he had in his locker were those textbooks over there and a windbreaker."

Nate shone his penlight into the duffel bag. It was empty—except for . . . "Hmm. Now what have we here?"

∞

"Where's Jamie?" Sondra asked, looking around. "She heard the ghost talking. I'm *serious!*"

Karine spotted her—"Jamie!"—and told Elisha, "Wait'll you hear what happened to her and Cindy Jenkins and Andy Bolland!"

Jamie was a tall girl, plainly dressed, who wore no makeup. Elisha had already seen her perform in drama class—she was good. She hurried over and took a chair next to Elisha.

"You met Elisha?" Sondra asked.

They introduced themselves.

"Tell her about that night in the Forbidden Hallway," said Karine, actually giddy about it.

Jamie gave Karine a kind but correcting look and then turned to Elisha. "You know which hall we're talking about?"

Elisha had heard a fresh report from Sondra and Karine—and had already learned of it at a family briefing the night before. "That rear hallway next to the gym."

"Some friends and I heard something in that hall. We were here one night for a rehearsal—"

SLAM! Every head in the lunchroom turned. Some big guy had just knocked Ian Snyder's books off the table, and now he was standing there smirking about it.

"Ohhh," said Karine, "don't pick on *him*. Anybody but *him!*"

❧

"What have you got?" Carrillo asked, stepping closer.

Nate prepared a plastic bag to receive the evidence, then pulled the duffel bag wide open and reached in with a pair of tweezers. "A soda straw."

Carrillo made a face. "A what?"

❧

Elijah saw the big guy slap Ian Snyder across the head, then do it again. He knew right away what was happening. "Who is that guy?"

"Leonard Baynes," said Trevor, hardly looking up. "He's always giving Snyder a hard time."

Elijah rose from his chair.

Carl grabbed his arm. "Hey, what are you doing?"

Elijah thought that was a silly question. "Somebody's getting hurt over there."

He walked down the row toward the trouble, and yes, there were plenty of eyes watching.

ᙍᙓ

"Hey," said Sondra, "isn't that your brother?"

Elisha saw Elijah's gait and the look in his eye. "Ohhh, that's him, all right." She knew what was coming and could only hope it wouldn't mess everything up.

"This could get ugly," said Karine.

LIES AND TERROR

LEONARD BAYNES WAS taunting Snyder, cursing him, slapping him. "Where's my ten dollars, freak? C'mon! Where's my ten dollars?"

Snyder said nothing and sat there taking it, angry but apparently helpless.

"Nice earring," said Baynes, reaching for it.

Elijah got right in the way. "Hi!" He stuck out his hand. "Elijah Springfield. This is my first day."

Baynes was twice as big as Elijah and he wasn't at all pleased with Elijah's timing. "Butt out."

 Baynes grabbed Elijah by the shoulder—"I said, butt out!"—and flung him into a row of students at the next table, spilling their food and knocking two of them over.

Elijah extended his hand toward Ian Snyder. "Elijah Springfield. And you are . . . ?"

Snyder was too startled to answer, much less shake hands.

Baynes grabbed Elijah by the shoulder— "I said, butt out!"— and flung him into a row of students at the next table, spilling their food and knocking two of them over.

Some cheers went up from the crowd. Some in the crowd whispered, looking scared. No one got up.

ॐ

"Oh, brother," said Carrillo. "Sounds like trouble in the lunchroom."

Nate only said, "Mmm" and continued examining the soda straw under a strong desk lamp. He held a magnifying glass in front of his eye and slowly moved along the length of the straw. He looked down one end and then down the other.

"What have you got?" Carrillo asked again.

The soda straw was common, typical, the same kind of straw one would find in any fast-food restaurant, in any grocery store.

And yet Nate was fascinated.

"Oh, maybe something," he said.

ॐ

"Where's a teacher?" Elisha cried, looking all around. "Where's Officer Carrillo?"

"You mean *Barney Fife?*" Karine giggled.

75

Elisha moaned, shook her head, and rose to her feet.

"What are you doing?" Karine squealed.

"I'm doing something about it," she answered, and started down the row. *This is not a convenient time to be wearing a skirt!* she thought.

※

Well, Elijah thought as he picked himself up, *at least he isn't picking on Snyder.* "Hey, come on now, I just want to be friends—"

Baynes tried to plant his big hand in Elijah's chest to shove him again—and immediately found himself slammed facedown on the table—right in front of Ian Snyder—his arm twisted in a hold that threatened to snap his elbow backward. It hurt.

"Please don't move," Elijah spoke into his ear. "If you move, your arm will break."

Baynes didn't move.

Now there were loud cheers and hoots from the crowd, enough to bring in a whole army of teachers, maybe even the vice principal.

※

Carrillo heard the commotion and had to tear himself away. "Gotta check this out."

"Mmm," said Nate.

Carrillo bolted from the room.

Nate shone a light up one end of the straw and looked down

76

the other. What was this inside the straw? It looked like sugar crystals. It couldn't be cocaine or methamphetamine, or Max would have smelled it. The straw did have a strange, musty smell. Sarah would have to see this.

⚬✕⚬

Elisha got there in time to hear Elijah's final words to Baynes: "We could start being friends right now or we can both get suspended. What'll it be?"

"Friends!" Elisha urged in a whisper, her body poised for the worst. "Just say it."

Baynes thought for only a moment. "Friends."

Elijah let him go, and he bolted from the scene red-faced and humiliated, brushing by Elisha and escaping through an outside exit door.

Elisha's whole body relaxed as a sigh of relief escaped her lungs.

⚬✕⚬

Officer Carrillo burst into the room looking for the trouble, whatever it was. All he saw were the two Springfield kids kneeling and bending, picking some scattered books and papers up off the floor, handing them to Ian Snyder.

"All right," he said, leaping upon the scene, "what's going on here?"

"We had a little collision," said Elijah. "Everybody's okay."

Carrillo looked at the kids' faces around the room. Most were expressing agreement, eyebrows cocked as if to say, "Yep, that's what it was," but some were smiling and snickering with a secret amusement, enough to make him suspicious.

"Well, okay," he said. "Clean it all up. And you watch yourself, Snyder!" He looked around the room. "And the rest of you get back to your lunch! You've only got five minutes!"

He began circling the room like a cop on a beat, in charge, eyes mean and wary.

&

Elijah handed the last of the scattered papers to Elisha, who then handed them to Ian Snyder. It gave Elisha a chance to see what Elijah had found: bizarre drawings of demons and occult symbols, poetry about blood and rituals, pages on witchcraft and spells downloaded from the Internet. Neither showed any reaction, but both saw it all.

"Anyway," Elijah said, extending his hand once again to Ian Snyder, "the name's Elijah."

Ian Snyder finished stashing everything back in his notebook, then shook Elijah's hand, the strange, animal look never leaving his eyes. "Ian Snyder—and thank you, but I fight my own battles."

Elijah shrugged. "Well, sorry, but I was raised to be there when a fellow human being needs help."

For the first time, the hint of a smile appeared at the corners of Snyder's mouth. "Leonard Baynes will be dealt with. Don't worry about that."

The bell rang and the great and instant exodus began. Elijah felt several friendly slaps on the back from students he didn't yet know. Snyder grabbed up his books and turned to leave. "But thanks anyway," he said over his shoulder.

Snyder was wearing a sleeveless shirt, and something on his shoulder caught Elijah's eye. Snyder had a tattoo.

A tattoo of an angel.

ꙩꙩ

In a quiet, neutral location—an RV park on the edge of town— the Springfields reviewed the day over dinner in the Holy Roller, a forty-foot motor home that served as home, office, and mobile crime lab.

Sarah examined the soda straw through the plastic bag, then opened the plastic bag and sniffed it for any odor. "You're right. There's a strange smell, kind of musty."

"Like an old basement or something," Nate commented.

"Yes, exactly." She sealed the bag again and set it aside. "The fact that the straw was buried under an athlete's laundry won't make the odor any easier to isolate."

Nate looked across the table at Elijah. "But we may have isolated the 'angel,' am I right?"

Since Elijah's mouth was full, Elisha spoke. "Ian Snyder has a reputation as a witch, and according to what we found in his books and papers today, hoo boy, he's into a *lot* of weird stuff."

Nate nodded. "He has a reputation around that school. Mr. Gessner and Officer Carrillo brought up his name yesterday."

"But here's the connection: The girls I talked to think he controls the ghost. Somehow he can get the ghost of Abel Frye to do his bidding."

Sarah recalled Jim Boltz's eerie cry, "The angel and Abel Frye."

"Sure. Exactly."

Elijah swallowed and spoke up. "He told me that Leonard Baynes—that's the bully we tangled with—'would be dealt with,' whatever that means."

"It means we'd better keep an eye on Leonard Baynes," said Nate. "But looking back on all this, we need to know if Snyder had anything against the first three victims."

"He did," said Elisha. "Sondra and Karine told me that all three of them used to pick on Snyder just as Baynes did today, and now . . ."

"Hold on," said Sarah. "This sounds like it's common knowledge among the student body."

Elisha shrugged. "It's no secret, that's for sure."

Sarah was astonished. "All this is happening right under the noses of the faculty, and they don't know about it?"

"They know about it," said Nate. "So I'm beginning to see what's frustrating Tom Gessner and bewildering the principal, Ms. Wyrthen. The school has metal detectors, a security officer, all the external, crime-stopping stuff, but who cares if some of the students are getting tormented and harassed? Sure, evil still gets through the doors, but at least there are no guns around."

"Nate . . ."

Nate forced the anger from his mind and took a moment to exhale his temper. "Anyway . . . It looks to me like Tom Gessner's theory is holding up. The victims have an enemy, maybe several enemies. But I'm not so sure about this witchcraft angle! It's too obvious, too easy—not to mention it's a touch unbelievable."

"And how do you prove a thing like witchcraft?" Elijah added.

"What's to prove?" said Sarah. "So far, all this talk about Abel Frye and witches could be nothing more than a silly craze that feeds on itself. I couldn't find any solid information anywhere on anyone named Abel Frye. Where'd the name come from? How do we know the kids didn't just make it up?"

"Mom," Elijah protested, "those guys in the hospital were saying his name!"

"So? They could be caught up in the same hysteria as all the others and blaming Abel Frye when the real blame lies somewhere else."

"That's where I'm going," Nate concurred. "You already have a ghost legend in place, and now there's Crystal Sparks' painting of the ghost that all the kids had to have seen."

"So I don't think we've found the truth yet. It's still hidden somewhere."

"It could be in that haunted hallway," Elisha offered. "I finally got the story from Jamie after the Leonard Baynes thing blew over. I'd really like to check out that hallway at night."

Nate asked, "And what do you expect to find?"

She shrugged. "Whatever Jamie, Cindy, and Andy thought was a ghost."

Elijah checked his watch. "It could be there right now."

Nate thought a moment. "You're going to stay in that hall-way, you understand? Don't wander into any rooms or closets or tight places where you don't have a clear safety zone around you."

Sarah concurred. "And take radios with you in case you need some help."

Nate looked at his watch. "I'll call Mr. Loman and see if he'll let you in."

Elijah and Elisha jumped up from the table, ready to go.

Late at night, with the lights out and no daylight coming through the windows, it became a cold, echoing, forbidding place where strange little sounds emerged out of the night silence and patches of light fell on walls, floor, and objects for no particular reason and with no discernible source.

"Take your homework!" Sarah advised firmly. "You *are* in school, remember! Oh—" She hurried into the lab at the back of the motor home and brought back a small but highly sophisticated digital recorder. "If you hear anything, I want to hear it, too."

⮾

During the day, Baker High School's back hallway was nothing more than a passage between the gym and the outside, a way to get from one place to another.

Late at night, with the lights out and no daylight coming through the windows, it became a cold, echoing, forbidding place where strange little sounds emerged out of the night silence and patches of light fell on walls, floor, and objects for no particular reason and with no discernible source. Elijah and Elisha were camped out near what used to be Jim Boltz's locker, studying by the light of small work lamps they wore on their heads. They had to leave the hallway dark because that was how it was "that night." How long they would have to wait was an open question, but they'd brought sleeping bags just in case.

Elijah glanced at his watch and spoke in a near whisper. "Nine-fifteen."

Elisha extinguished her light and looked up and down the dark hallway. "Jamie said they heard the ghost about nine o'clock."

"Where?"

She nodded toward Jim Boltz's locker. "Right about here."

Elijah raised his head, directing his work lamp upward where it illumined the little hanging man scratched on the locker door. "Well . . . so far he's been pretty quiet."

His backpack was beside him. He reached into it and took out the digital recorder their mother had sent with them. "What do you think?"

She shrugged, a dark silhouette against a gray patch of light upon the floor. "Now's as good a time as any."

Elijah consulted a piece of paper Mr. Loman had given them when he let them in: the combination to Jim Boltz's locker. He stood, dialed the combination, and opened the locker door. Then, with double-backed tape, he fastened the little recorder to the inside of the locker's air vent. He clicked it on, and a tiny red light appeared. "Okay, we're rolling." He closed the door and spun the lock.

The recorder was a highly sensitive device that could record continuously for twenty-four hours. Even if no "ghost" made a sound that night, they still had a backup, an electronic ear listening around the clock. The plan was to replace the memory card with a blank one each day, and then review each day's recording. Maybe, just maybe, they would record something unusual.

Elijah rested his back against the locker and went back to his studies. Elisha clicked her light on again and did the same.

"So what do you think of your humanities class?" she asked.

Elijah had to chuckle. "Mr. Carlson keeps shooting himself in the foot."

She cocked her head and gave him a testing look. "Elijah. You aren't being difficult, are you?"

He raised his eyebrows innocently. "What? He was telling us there's no right or wrong, and I just asked him if that statement was right or wrong, that's all."

She laughed. "You're going to get us kicked out of here."

"Ohhh?" he asked with mock indignity. "So how are things going in biology?"

"It's all coming back to me. I think Mom made it more interesting, but Mr. Harrigan's really nice . . ." She looked toward the ceiling. "And I hope he stays that way tomorrow. We have to discuss this chapter on evolution." She opened her biology textbook and showed him a page.

He whistled in amazement. "The *Miller* experiment? That's still in the textbooks?"

"And the Ernst Haeckel embryos . . ."

"You've got to be kidding!"

She showed him the pages to prove it. "*And* the whale that evolved from a cow."

Elijah saw the diagrams and the paragraphs and had to chuckle. "What are you going to do?"

"Well . . . Mr. Harrigan seems like a nice man. Maybe I can talk to him in private."

"Yeah. Good idea."

She looked up and down the hall. "I'm getting sleepy."

They closed their textbooks and clicked off their lights, then sat in the dark and the silence. Occasionally, they could hear the low, distant roar of a car passing on the road outside and see the dim reflection of its headlights moving along the wall. A tiny, living thing was moving behind the lockers somewhere. They could hear the faint scratching of its toenails. The furnace kicked on and the sound of moving air filled the hallway. With some imagination they could hear a voice in that wind, even imagine a melody.

But until ten o'clock, when they finally wriggled into their sleeping bags, there were no unusual sounds, no voices, no ghost.

When Mr. Loman awoke them early the next morning, they felt disappointed and even a little foolish.

∽

A little irritable, too. Besides coming up empty on their "ghost-hunting," they'd gone without adequate sleep, which made them both a touch less patient in their classes.

Mr. Harrigan was a younger man, quite good-looking and mild-mannered, and Elisha did not want a confrontation with him. But when he sat on the edge of his desk and told the class, "All right, let's open up the book to chapter four and discuss evolution," she just knew she'd have to say something.

Especially when Mr. Harrigan asked for it. "First thing I'd like to ask is, Did anyone have any trouble with this chapter? Did anything bother you about it?"

Elisha raised her hand, but so did another girl toward the back.

Mr. Harrigan called on the other girl. "Yes, Tracy."

Tracy looked puzzled. "Mr. Harrigan, if whales evolved from four-legged animals, isn't that like evolution going backward? I mean, at the beginning of the chapter it says that all life began in the sea and then crawled up on the land, but now they're saying that an animal turned into a whale and crawled back into the ocean."

Mr. Harrigan just raised an eyebrow. "Well? The book says it happened. And what about the bones near the whale's tail? The book says those bones used to be a pelvis when the whale had legs."

Tracy shrugged. "Well, I just don't get it, that's all."

Elisha shot her hand up again.

Mr. Harrigan smiled, amused at her impatience. "Go ahead."

"The bones near the whale's tail aren't the remains of a pelvis! They have to do with the reproductive organs."

Mr. Harrigan raised that eyebrow again. "But the book says those bones used to be a pelvis when the whale was a four-legged animal."

Elisha paged through the chapter. "Then why doesn't the book show us the fossil of an animal with fins, or a whale with legs? And Tracy's right: Evolution is supposed to mean that something is getting better, *gaining* something like legs, not *losing* them."

Mr. Harrigan kept smiling as if amused. "Looks like you had a little trouble with this chapter."

Well, he did open the door, she thought. Elisha jumped through it. "I had a *lot* of trouble with this chapter!" She flipped to a page so fast she almost tore it. "Like this whole thing about the embryos of different animals all looking the same, so that's supposed to prove they all had a common ancestor, and even *human* embryos having gill slits as if they're somehow related to fish—that's a fraud! Ernst Haeckel created these phony drawings clear back in the 1860s, and his university found the whole thing to be a fraud in 1874! This is a bald-faced *lie!*"

Mr. Harrigan looked alarmed. "A lie, Miss Springfield?"

The whole class was looking at her, but she didn't care. "Yes, Mr. Harrigan. A lie. Just like this other part that says the Miller experiment created life in the laboratory. Miller did no such thing. He zapped some gases—what were they?" She read from the text. "'Methane, ammonia, water vapor, and hydrogen.' He zapped them with electricity to simulate lightning and tried to get them to form amino acids."

"Well, they did form amino acids, didn't they?"

Elisha strained her brain to remember the details. "A few amino acids don't make a protein!" She used to know a lot more about this, but now she was drawing a blank and it was very frustrating.

Mr. Harrigan chuckled. "I guess you *did* have trouble with this chapter!"

A fellow across the room raised his hand.

"Yes, Eric."

The whole class was looking

at her, but she didn't care.

Eric's response had a snide tone. "I think she just needs to read a little better. Getting back to the whales . . ." He read from the text, "'The whales have a vestigial pelvis, just like humans have a vestigial tail.'"

A few kids chuckled. Not Elisha. She was crabby to begin with, but that really set her off. "A tail!? You think humans used to have *tails?*"

Eric looked incredulous that anyone would question such an idea. "I can *read!*" He pointed at the text in front of him. "It says right here that we don't need those bones at the base of our spine. They're just left over from when we were monkeys."

She turned in her desk and glared at him. "Those bones support the muscles that keep you from pooping in your pants, in case you didn't know! But if you think you don't need yours . . ." She groped in her handbag and pulled out her wallet. "I will gladly pay for you to have yours removed!"

The whole class fell apart with laughter.

"All right, all right," Mr. Harrigan cautioned, but even he was laughing.

Suddenly a voice piped up from the rear of the classroom. "If I may volunteer something?"

Mr. Harrigan seemed glad for the help. "Yeah, go ahead, Norman."

Norman Bloom, a thin, pimple-faced kid with thick glasses and obvious brainpower, was Mr. Harrigan's T.A., his teaching assistant. Most of the T.A.s at Baker were students a grade or two ahead of the class in which they assisted. He'd been arranging plants on the shelves in the back, but now he was thumbing through the class textbook. "Getting back to the Miller experiment, that girl up front . . ."

"Elisha," she told him.

"Elisha is right about the Miller experiment. The book says Miller created life in the laboratory, but all he really created was a bunch of problems. The experiment produced a few amino acids, but it mostly produced tar and carboxylic acid, and those are poisonous to life. He left oxygen out of the mix because oxygen would have broken down the amino acids, but there was oxygen on the earth when life was supposed to have formed. Even if there was no oxygen, then there couldn't have been any ozone layer, so the UV rays from the sun would have killed every living cell anyway. He had to isolate the amino acids artificially to keep them from breaking apart again, and anyway, they never would have bonded to each other to start forming a protein because they would have bonded to the tar or the carboxylic acid first." He shook his head. "The experiment was a flop. It didn't prove anything."

The class sat in dumb silence. This Norman was one bright kid. They looked at Mr. Harrigan to see what he would say.

"Norman," he finally answered, "you and Elisha are absolutely right."

The kids in the class stared at each other. Was their biology teacher actually saying—

"The people who wrote this textbook are either sorely misinformed, or they are dishonest."

There was stunned silence. Elisha gave Norman a thumbs-up and he returned it.

"You mean," said Tracy, weakly turning the pages, "it isn't true?"

Eric piped up, "Mr. Harrigan, you're not supposed to teach religion in school."

"Have you heard me say one thing about religion?"

He got silence for an answer. He started paging through the chapter. "The chart showing the embryos looking similar during development—page forty-seven—is a fraud. The Miller experiment on page fifty proved nothing, and every honest scientist will admit that. As for four-legged mammals evolving into whales . . ." They waited for his answer. "That's pure fantasy, pure imagination. There isn't one shred of scientific evidence that it ever happened, nor is there any proof that birds evolved from dinosaurs. As for the statement on page forty-five, 'The first living cells emerged 3.8 billion to 4 billion years ago,' just look at what it says next: 'There is no record of the event.'" He almost laughed again. "They say there is no record of the event, so . . . come on . . . ," he prodded.

"So how do they know it happened 3.8 to 4 billion years ago?" Elisha offered.

"Exactly. They don't know." He stood to his feet and started walking around the class, the textbook in his hand. "Ladies and gentlemen, I want to impress upon you that evolution is a *theory* with many unanswered questions—and a lot of wishful thinking, I might add. I'm not here to erase or debunk the theory, or even come near preaching religion, but I'm not going to lie to you, either. I'll tell you what we know for sure, and those of you who want an A in this class will have to show me that you've checked it out for yourself. Now for your next assignment . . ."

Elisha relaxed in her desk, warmed with encouragement. Where did this school ever find a teacher like Mr. Harrigan?

ೞ

Leonard Baynes was a junior, a poor student, not good-looking, and generally unhappy. His life at home was miserable, he found it hard to fit in anywhere at school, he was not athletic, and he excelled at very little except for one thing: being tough. Of course, he could only be tough by pushing around smaller, weaker students who didn't have the strength to fight back, but so what? At least he could be better than *somebody* at *something*.

Slapping Ian Snyder around had become a regular pastime, and Leonard could even justify it by reminding himself that Ian Snyder was weird. Weird people deserved to be slapped around. They asked for it. There were plenty of other guys who slapped them around. It was an okay thing to do.

But things took a bad turn yesterday at lunchtime, and word had gotten to the guys in wood shop. While he worked at his station, sanding the side panel of a cabinet, he could hear and see the same cruel tidbit being passed from classmate to classmate, from the drill press to the drafting table to the power planer: Baynes got whipped by a math geek. They were all snickering and looking at him.

Then came the little jabs from the boys who were tougher than he was: "Heard you got decked by a geek, Baynes." "How's your arm, Baynes? Did that little squirt break it?"

He said nothing back. What *could* he say? He couldn't slug them because they could slug him back. All he could do was try to concentrate on his work and mutter cusswords to himself.

They started talking about Ian Snyder.

"Hey," one of them said, "maybe that geek is the ghost!" They all laughed.

"Hey, I know," said another. "Snyder put a spell on him."

"Yeah," said a third, "turned him into a girl."

They had a good laugh at that one, too.

Leonard could feel his face heating up, turning red with a double anger: anger because they were laughing at him, but on top of that, anger because he couldn't do anything about it.

He heard one of the guys say, "Don't laugh. You don't know what that Snyder can do." He was serious.

Leonard's hands started to shake. He could feel a twisting pain deep in his guts. Something else was flaring up inside him.

He felt afraid.

Afraid of what? The ghost? A spell? He started having flashbacks of that moment in the lunchroom, a slow-motion replay. He didn't remember the face of the geek very well, but the sinister face of Ian Snyder he couldn't get out of his mind: that weird black hair, that grayish complexion, and those eyes! The whole time Leonard was slapping Snyder around, those eyes showed no anger or fear—only a dangerous, sinister control. Snyder was muttering something. What was it, a curse?

Leonard tried to shake off the fear, but it kept coming back. He tried to keep sanding his project, but his hands were getting weak and unsteady.

Some guy at the drafting table was talking in hushed tones with his buddies, talking about *him,* talking about Snyder, the geek, and then Leonard heard the name "... Abel Frye ..."

He froze right there, his whole body shaking, glaring at his mockers, wanting to throw something, wanting to grab them, wanting to run. *Don't say that name! What do you want to do, bring the ghost in here?*

They must have seen the fear in his eyes. Some looked afraid themselves, but some mocked him all the more. "What's the matter, Baynes? Afraid of ghosts?"

All he could do was curse them at the top of his voice.

They sent his cursings right back, getting a big kick out of the whole thing.

> They must have seen the fear in his eyes. Some looked afraid themselves, but some mocked him all the more. "What's the matter, Baynes? Afraid of ghosts?"

Mr. Tyler, the wood shop instructor, heard it. "Hey, is there a problem over there?"

The mockers turned back to their work. Leonard tried to do the same but couldn't.

"Baynes?" Mr. Tyler called sternly. His voice sounded far away to Leonard, not really in Leonard's world. "Baynes! I'm talking to you!"

Leonard looked around frantically, especially toward the ceiling. Something was coming into the room. He could feel it. It was coming in like smoke through all the cracks. It was coming for him. He dropped his sanding block, backing away.

Was this the ghost of Abel Frye? Is this what happened to the others? The guys had spoken the name. They'd *called* this thing in here. They were saying things about him, letting the ghost know who he was, where he was.

Mr. Tyler was lecturing him, but his stern, corrective words only flitted around the room like bats, never landing. The *thing*, the *ghost,* was filling the room. Leonard couldn't breathe. He could feel pins sticking him all over his body.

Then, like an image projected on a sheet of smoke, a face appeared. A dead thing. Gray, with black, sunken eyes. A hawk on the shoulder. Just like the painting.

He bolted, ran for the door, dodging around a worktable, slipping on some sawdust, almost falling, running into someone, running some more.

"Baynes!" he heard Mr. Tyler holler.

He was out the door, out of his mind.

5

THE FORBIDDEN
HALLWAY

IT ALL STARTED WITH the Ten Commandments. Mr. Carlson, Elijah's humanities teacher, was commenting on a recent court decision that required a small town in Indiana to remove the Ten Commandments from the lawn in front of its courthouse.

"What makes this a good decision is that it once again upholds the whole idea of tolerance and multiculturalism in our society," he was saying. "Posting the Ten Commandments on any public building is nothing more than the state imposing religious dogma on the people, asserting that one religious viewpoint is superior to all others. And even if we didn't consider the religious part of it, it would still mean the state was imposing a certain morality, and that would be wrong as well. Truth should be left up to the individual. *Right* and *wrong* should be left up to the individual."

Elijah raised his hand. He just couldn't help it.

Mr. Carlson cringed a cringe the whole class could see. "Yes, Mr. Springfield, what is it this time?"

"You're saying that it's wrong to impose morality on people?"

He sighed. "Yes. I hope I've made that clear."

"Then how can you say it's *wrong* to impose morality? You can't say something is wrong if it's wrong to say something is wrong."

The class snickered, something Mr. Carlson detested.

"Mr. Springfield, does it ever occur to you Bible advocates that the posting of the Ten Commandments might make others uncomfortable?"

"Are you saying there's something wrong with that?"

Mr. Carlson laughed, the hint of a sneer on his face. "Oh, no! You're not going to suck me into a morality debate. I said right and wrong should be left up to the individual and I'll stand on that."

"Well, I don't think you believe what you're saying."

"Well, of course I do, and so should you." He looked at the rest of the class. "Now, as far as the court ruling applies—"

"Uh, excuse me?"

Mr. Carlson only simmered and nodded to him.

"Mr. Carlson, you keep using the word *should*. Truth, and right and wrong, *should* be left up to the individual; I *should* believe what you're saying. I *should*. Doesn't that mean you're imposing your morals on me, your sense of what I should and should not do?"

"I'm telling you what's right. That's my job, my duty!"

"So what if I don't see it your way? Am I wrong?"

"In this case, of course you are."

"Then you don't believe right and wrong should be left up to the individual."

"Oh, yes I do! I believe all viewpoints are equally valid."

"With all due respect, sir, no, you don't."

Mr. Carlson sat on the edge of his desk, a smug expression coming over his face. "Mr. Springfield. How can you say I believe something other than what I say I believe?"

"Because if you really believed that all viewpoints are equally valid, you wouldn't be arguing with me."

"I'm not arguing with you."

"Yes, you are."

"No, I'm not!"

"Yes, you are."

"No, I'm—!" The whole class was laughing by now, so Mr. Carlson ended *that* little exchange and shifted gears. "Class, be mindful now, that Mr. Springfield is a Christian. Now, I'm not knocking that. That's his right, his privilege. But we have to be careful: Anytime a person argues from strong, personal convictions, you have to question the way he sees things."

A voice came from the back. "Then we should question *you*."

"But *I'm* not speaking from personal convictions."

"Then Springfield's right. You don't really believe what you're saying."

Mr. Carlson only smirked.

"That's my whole point," said Elijah. "You don't believe what you're telling us."

"So why should we listen to you?" came the voice in the back.

100

"Oh, but you're wrong," said Mr. Carlson. "I *do* believe it!"

"Then you're speaking from conviction," said Elijah.

"No, I'm not!"

"And you're telling us we're wrong!" said the voice. "I thought that was up to us to decide."

"I'm not—" The class was laughing again. Mr. Carlson's face was getting red. He started over. "Listen. I'm simply saying that it's wrong to think one person's viewpoint is morally superior to any other person's viewpoint."

The voice piped up, "See? You're saying something is wrong."

Now Mr. Carlson was angry and didn't try to hide it. "Of course I am! Absolutely!"

Elijah had to laugh. "So now you believe in *absolutes*."

"I do *not!*"

"But you do think your viewpoint is superior to ours?" came the voice.

Mr. Carlson held out his hand, palm outward. "Ohhh, no. You're not going to get me making value judgments. I'm not falling for that!"

"So I guess you won't be grading our papers either," said Elijah, and the whole classroom broke into cheers and applause.

Mr. Carlson didn't think that was funny. He rose to his feet, his expression grim, and said, "Well, there is one absolute I believe in right now, Mr. Springfield, and that is that you are absolutely going to be here after school today and make up for every minute you have taken from our class time with this silly debate!"

Elijah wasn't surprised. He'd asked for it.

Then Mr. Carlson said, "And you, too, Snyder! *Be here,* right after school!"

Elijah spun in his desk and looked.

Yes. It was Ian Snyder, the voice from the back of the room, slouching in his seat defiantly but giving Elijah the secretive smile of a comrade.

ᑫᕙᑐ

Sarah Springfield winced just a little when she got the phone call from Elijah. "So did he say how long he was going to keep you?"

"I don't know."

She drew a patient breath and sighed it out. "I do hope you were respectful."

"Yes, ma'am, I was. But . . . it *was* a debate, and we, uh, we were both pretty firm in our positions."

"Oh, dear."

"But guess what? Ian Snyder got into it, too, and he was on my side! So now he has to stay after school with me. Isn't that just like something the Lord would do?"

She stifled a laugh as she shook her head. "God does work in wondrous ways. Well, listen to me: You follow Mr. Carlson's wishes, do you hear? He's still in authority."

"I will. Gotta go."

"Good-bye."

Sarah and Nate were back in the lab section of the motor

home, a room filled with flasks, test tubes, bottles, gizmos, and electronic instruments. Nate was just putting a memory card into the computer as Sarah hung up the phone. "I guess it's our own doing. We taught them how to think."

"I just hope he showed proper respect," she said, sitting at the lab table across from him.

"Don't worry. We'll get a full report." He clicked the computer mouse and selected the tiny memory card. "Here's the recording of the Forbidden Hallway from last night. I've cued it up to where the kids finally sacked out."

Sarah resumed her chemical analysis of the soda straw. "Thank you very much. Could you put it on fast speed? I'll listen while I'm working."

The telephone rang again. Nate picked it up. "Springfield."

Sarah glanced at Nate's face, then looked again. Nate's face told her he was listening to serious news. "How long ago?" he asked. "Okay, I'm on my way." He hung up and grabbed his coat. "That was Tom Gessner. We might have another victim."

"Oh, no . . ."

"I'm going to meet him at the hospital. I'll call as soon as I can."

He went out the door.

"We might have another victim."

❦

Mr. Carlson was still in a sour mood. "Gentlemen, you owe me ten minutes of silence. You will sit in your seats and you will not say a word. If you speak one word, you will remain here one more minute. Two words, two minutes. Three words, three minutes, and so on."

Elijah had a question and raised his hand.

"No, Mr. Springfield! There will be no opportunity for questions! Ten minutes of silence." He looked at the clock on the wall. "Starting now."

Mr. Carlson sat at his desk in front of the room and busied himself with correcting papers.

Mr. Carlson had placed them in desks right next to each other. Perhaps this was his way of placing them in the path of temptation: They were sitting right next to each other but couldn't say a word. That could be tough.

❦

Since her brother was staying after school, Elisha decided to do the same, dropping in on Norman Bloom in the bio-chem stockroom. As Mr. Harrigan's T.A., Norman spent a few minutes at the end of every school day taking care of the lab rats, lab mice, insects in jars, Floyd the boa constrictor, and Jesse the white rabbit. Right now he was dividing the lab mice among new, clean cages, picking them up gently by their tails.

"This one's Fergie," he said, setting the mouse in its new cage. "He's gone through the maze faster than any of his brothers and sisters. Of course, that could be because he's a teacher's pet and Mr. Harrigan gives him more chances than anybody else."

Elisha took a close look at Floyd the boa constrictor, curled up in his glass terrarium. "So what does he eat—or dare I ask?"

Norman shrugged apologetically. "Any mice that can't figure out the maze."

She shuddered. "I thought so."

"But, hey, watch this."

He wiggled his finger above the mouse named Fergie, then whistled a short little tune. Fergie rose up on his haunches and, following Norman's finger, danced in a little circle.

Elisha was enchanted. "How did you get him to do that?"

Norman tossed Fergie a kernel of corn. "Oh, a little love and attention can go a long way." Then he added, "Too bad more people don't realize that."

☙❧

Sarah had cut the soda straw into one-inch lengths and run chemical tests on several of them. So far she'd managed to identify the white crystals inside the straw: common sugar, but with some other strange compound added. It was the unknown compound she was trying to identify now. It might be a hallucinogenic drug, or nothing more serious than a candy flavoring. She should know soon enough.

On the desk behind her, the computer was replaying one long, continuous, hissing sound—the sound of a silent hallway many times normal speed. It wasn't very exciting. She could recognize the sound of passing vehicles on the road outside—they sounded like little bees buzzing by—and the sound of the school's big furnace turning on and off—that sounded like waves of the ocean crashing very, very slowly. Every once in a while there would be a sound like someone running their thumbnail along the teeth of a comb and it made her laugh. Even at fast speed she could recognize the sound: Elijah was snoring.

She took a scraping from the inside of one of the soda straw sections and placed it on a microscope slide. She prepared to stain it.

A new sound came out of the computer. Like a distant machine running. Faint. Rhythmical. Repetitive. She reached over, hit the stop button, scanned the track backward, hit the play button.

Nothing but hiss, then another vehicle passing, and then . . . there it was. The same thing, over and over.

She cued the track backward and played it again at normal speed.

☙❧

Elijah thought it would be worthwhile at least to make eye contact with Ian. Ian looked back at him, and his eyes were actually friendly.

Elijah smiled and gave a little nod.

Ian smiled back and gave Elijah a look that said, "You were good today."

Elijah pointed at Ian, then held up two fingers: "You, too."

Mr. Carlson looked up from his work and they quit signaling.

∞

Elisha watched with wonder—and a touch of squeamishness—as Norman draped Floyd the boa constrictor over his shoulders and let Floyd wrap himself around Norman's arms. "Wow. You, uh, you sure have a way with animals."

Norman returned Floyd's gaze as the snake raised its head and came eye to eye with him. "I saw a guy do this in Africa."

Elisha was impressed. "You've been to Africa?"

Norman began easing Floyd back into his terrarium. "My dad spent a year in Kenya for his company—they explore for oil and minerals, things like that. So I got to spend the summer with him. I like Africa. You can meet all the animals you want over there."

"That's wonderful. It really is."

Norman glanced at a computer in the corner, the screen glowing with a jungle animals screensaver. "So's the Internet. Anything you want to know about animals and insects, anywhere in the world, you can find out. I got a recipe for a really great granola for mice off this thing."

Elisha looked at her watch. "Well, Elijah ought to be out of the penalty box by now."

Norman chuckled. "He actually took on Carlson. You're brave, you two."

She wasn't sure what to say. "We don't mean to cause trouble. I guess we just have this thing about the truth."

Norman placed some lettuce in Jesse the rabbit's cage and closed the cage door. "I admire that. We shouldn't be afraid of the truth—even if it pokes holes in our pet theories."

She picked up her books. "It was nice to meet you."

He smiled. "The pleasure was mine, really. See you tomorrow."

ෲ

Sarah turned up the volume on the computer's sound system and hit the play button again. The track played at normal speed. She leaned toward the sound, her eyes closed, and listened. Something was there, barely audible, layered beneath the quiet rush of air through the school's heating ducts. It sounded like a voice, or maybe voices. It ended. She cued the track back and played it again.

Aaa . . . Ahhh . . . Aaaa . . . Aaa . . . Ahhh . . . Aaaa . . .

Like a chant. But was it just something in the rushing air? Was she imagining it?

The computer had its own equalizer. She clicked the mouse, brought it on-screen, and began adjusting the frequencies, filtering out all the sounds around *the* sound, bringing it to the forefront.

Ehhhh . . . Ahhhrrr . . . Aaaaaannn . . .

Her stomach twisted and she felt a chill. She played it again, studying a graphic sound wave on the computer screen, reducing some of the highs, dropping out the lows, turning up the midrange where the sound was.

Lehhhh . . . nahhhrrr . . . Baaaannnn . . . sss . . .

A voice speaking a name over and over.

The phone rang and she jumped an inch off her chair. Gasping for a few stable breaths, she grabbed the receiver. "Hello."

ᘓᘔ

Nate was at the hospital, in the hall just outside the room where the first three victims lay. "Sarah, we have another victim. They just brought him in."

"Leonard Baynes?"

Nate looked through the door into the room where doctors and nurses were holding Leonard Baynes down, trying to sedate him and tie him to the bed. He was screaming, grappling, staring wide-eyed at unseen terrors. "That's right. It's . . . it's terrible. I can't begin to describe it." He turned away. He had no doubts that Sarah could hear the screams coming from the room. "Tom Gessner is here. He's trying to take care of Leonard's mother." Just a few yards down the hall, Gessner sat on a couch with Mrs. Baynes, speaking words of comfort and obviously trying to keep her under control. She was almost as frantic as Leonard. Nate asked, "How did you know it was Leonard Baynes?"

Sarah stared at the computer, half-covering her mouth with

her free hand as the *sound* continued to pulse from the speakers. "A . . . a little ghost told me."

ᴄ✕ᴐ

Night. The hallway dark. Nerves on edge. So quiet they could monitor the volume and tempo of their own breathing, they could hear their hearts beating in their chests, they could sense the tone of the air within the hallway's four surfaces, like the ever-present rumble of air in a monstrous culvert.

Nate stood at the corner of the gym, the entrance to this hallway, peering through night-vision goggles. Through the goggles, the hallway was an eerie world of green shades and shadows, the windows dark, the lockers glaring, the floor mottled with patches of light and shadow.

Some thirty feet from Nate's position, his back against the

At the far end of the hall, silhouetted against the big double exit doors, Sarah waited, watched, and listened, night goggles and headphones making her look like a big insect.

110

lockers, Mr. Loman stood motionless—except for the steady sweep of his eyes, now wide with foreboding. Farther down, Tom Gessner stood against the windows, listening, just listening. Halfway down, Elijah sat perfectly still in the center of the hall, headphones on his ears, manning a soundboard and recorder. The recorder was already running, making a digital record through four separate microphones positioned in strategic places up and down the hallway.

Just beyond him, Elisha sat with her back against the locker that used to belong to Jim Boltz. This was where the first recording was made. She slept through the first one; she wouldn't be sleeping this time. She was wearing her head-mounted light, but had it turned off for now.

At the far end of the hall, silhouetted against the big double exit doors, Sarah waited, watched, and listened, night goggles and headphones making her look like a big insect.

Nate's mind kept racing, going over things. They'd emptied Leonard Baynes' locker immediately, but found nothing—yet—that clarified just what they were dealing with. The locker had been marked, however, with that same cryptic symbol of the little hanging man, the symbol of Abel Frye. With Mr. Loman's help, they'd checked every other locker in the school for the same symbol, but found nothing. The theory that this might be sabotage of Baker's football team was in question—Leonard Baynes was no athlete.

The possibility that Ian Snyder had anything to do with this was practically a no-brainer, but they still needed some kind of direct proof. They needed to *know*.

Ten-thirty. Every passing vehicle on the road outside was a nuisance. The sound overpowered everything else, and came through the headphones so loudly that Elijah and Sarah had to momentarily hold the earphones away from their ears.

No talking. No walking. Whatever it was, they wanted to hear it. They didn't want *it* to hear *them*.

The furnace kicked on and air began to rush through the heating ducts. Sarah and Elijah winced. Another nuisance noise, but there wasn't much they could do about it. The building had to be heated. Not a big problem, though; the voices had come through the other night even though the furnace was running.

Ten-forty. Another vehicle passed. Sarah and Elijah lifted their earphones away. The sound faded; they set the phones back in place.

Clunk.

Their eyes opened—wide. What was that?

Elijah put his hand up to signal the others, using his free hand to press an earphone close to his ear. Every person in the hall froze. Every breath became shallow and silent.

Elijah and Sarah pressed the earphones against their ears, straining to hear.

A swishing, a scraping. Movement.

Mr. Loman clamped his arms in front of him, afraid he would start trembling. He *thought* he heard something.

Nate and Sarah carefully scanned the hallway through their goggles, every inch of it, looking for anything strange, any movement at all. So far, nothing.

Elisha braced herself against the locker and slowly moved her head about, sampling every direction for sounds. *Come on, Abel. Come on.*

Mr. Gessner was standing so still it was easy to forget he was even there.

Elijah and Sarah heard it first. A faraway moan, low and mournful. Long, drawn-out vowels as if singing . . .

Ahhhhh . . . naaaaahhhhh . . . Iiilllll . . . Errrr . . .

Elijah tried to read Mr. Gessner's face in the dark. He finally moved, if only an inch. He was listening. He could hear it.

Sssshhhhaahhhhh . . . Naaaaa . . . Mmiiiiillllll . . . Errrrr . . .

Mr. Loman crossed himself. He was hearing it, too.

Nate began to move down the hall ever so slowly, listening, scanning. Sarah started moving in from the other direction.

Elisha wasn't as frightened as she was astounded. It was the perfect ghostly sound. It seemed to come from everywhere, all around them.

Nate reached Mr. Loman, who actually grabbed his arm for steadiness, for support.

There was no mistaking it now. It was a voice, a slow, mournful voice coming from all around them, faint but filling the hall.

Mr. Gessner began to move away from the windows toward the center of the hallway. Then he knelt down and put his ear to the floor. The way he jerked his head up from the floor and looked at them told them he'd found something.

Elisha put her ear to the floor. *Yes! We're tracking you down, Abel!*

Mr. Loman put his ear to the wall, then signaled wildly with his hand.

Nate put his ear to the wall. *Yes, there it was.*

And the words were more distinct: *Shahhhh . . . nahhhh . . . mmiiiilllllllllerrrr . . .*"

"Shawna Miller," Gessner whispered.

"The old building!" Loman whispered to Nate. Nate leaned close. Loman had his full attention. "This hallway is built over the site of the old building, the old basement and foundation. The plumbing runs through there, the heating, everything. That's what's carrying the sound up here!"

Nate tore off his goggles. "How do we get down there?"

Mr. Loman wagged his head, his eyes wide with wonder and fear. "I—I don't know. I've never been down there. I thought it was all filled in, you know, closed off."

Nate signaled Elisha, who tiptoed silently to them, carrying a set of blueprints. Nate unrolled the page he wanted, scanned it under the beam of Elisha's headlamp, and said, "Okay." He pointed to a location on the blueprint. "Around the back."

Sarah passed her night goggles to Elijah and took charge of the recording, freeing him to go with the others as they stole out of the building through the big exit doors. The exit doors were noisy no matter how careful they tried to be, closing with a heavy thud, the lock rod falling into place with a loud, metallic clank.

The voice stopped, just like that.

Better hurry, Sarah thought.

ᗡᘒᗡ

Nate, Elijah and Elisha, Mr. Gessner, and Mr. Loman hurried around the back of the building, trying to be as quiet as possible as they maneuvered through a maintenance alley and into a fenced-in parking area for Dumpsters, packing crates, scenery from several years of drama productions, and the school's two maintenance trucks.

Mr. Loman came to a halt, puffing from the exertion and looking about frantically. "I don't know," he said in a hushed, desperate voice. "Like I say, it's all built over, it's filled in."

Nate looked at the blueprints again. "Easy now, just take it easy. Show me where the new building starts in relation to the old one. Where is this wall right here?"

Mr. Loman looked at the plans, then waved his hand toward the rear wall of the gymnasium. "This wall runs right along the top of the old one, but"—he pointed at the plans—"that corner isn't there anymore and this section of the old basement . . . well, I guess they filled it in."

"You *guess?*"

"I . . . I don't know."

Nate was already looking beyond the fence as he thought aloud. "That much crawlspace had to have some ventilation somewhere."

Beyond the fence were bushes, young trees, wild growth. He hurried out of the parking area and around to the other side of the fence as the others followed.

He stopped short, motioned for a halt, then pointed.

This ground had been tramped on quite regularly. There was a path of compacted earth and sparse grass leading into the bushes.

Nate led the way, moving slowly, pushing the branches of the young trees aside, pressing ahead through the low growth. They penetrated several yards into the thicket before Nate halted again.

His flashlight now shone on some old boards. They were uncovered and clean although the surrounding ground was covered with old leaves and twigs. Obviously, they'd been placed there recently. Nate stooped down and pulled a board aside.

There was a dark space underneath.

They all pitched in and cleared the boards away. Now they were peering into a narrow hole in the ground, a hand-dug excavation that uncovered a buried concrete wall.

"The old building came out this far," whispered Nate. "This is the old basement wall."

In the center of the wall was a square opening, an old vent just large enough for a lean-bodied person to crawl through.

Nate looked at Elijah and Elisha. "No heroics, now."

Without another word, Elijah dropped into the hole, exchanging the night goggles for a headlamp he took from his belt. He handed the night goggles up to his father. Elisha dropped into the hole beside him.

As they both looked through the opening, their headlamps illumined what had once been a basement, now filled with

rubble, broken concrete, and dangerous tangles of steel rein-
forcement rod. They could see gaps and cavities in the debris,
large enough for a daring person to pass through. From deep
inside the earth came the low rumble of the school's furnace.

Elijah took Elisha's hand, and she reached up and took her
father's hand.

"Dear Lord," Nate prayed, "we pray for Your watchcare over
us, for safety, and for wisdom. Amen."

"Amen," the kids whispered.

Elijha crawled through, and Elisha followed.

They were inside.

6

WITCHES AND
BULLIES

THE AIR SMELLED MUSTY, like an old cellar, and dusty, like the pulverized concrete that lay everywhere. In here, the throbbing of the school's furnace was more than a sound; it was a presence. Space to turn was tight. Standing in here was like being buried alive under an old structure that had fallen in on itself.

In the beams of their headlamps, a narrow, haphazard path wound through helter-skelter slabs of concrete and disappeared into a bramble of tumbled concrete posts and ceiling-high piles of rubble. Elisha tapped Elijah's side and pointed toward the floor, now a thick layer of grayish grit and dust. There were footprints in the dust, some of them perfect impressions of popular shoe soles, the brand names readable. The most recent prints were heading the opposite direction—*out,* in other words.

"Looks like we missed them," Elisha whispered.

Elijah turned toward the opening through which they'd come. Their father was standing just outside. "Somebody just scrambled out of here. We've got some footprints," he reported.

Their father handed a camera through the opening and Elijah snapped several pictures. As near as they could tell, five people had just come through here.

By now, Sarah had arrived with two radios with headsets. She passed them down to Nate, who passed them through the vent. Elijah and Elisha clipped the radios to their belts and put on the headsets over their headlamps, an earphone for one ear, a tiny microphone to the side of their mouths. "Hello. Hello," Elijah said.

"We read you loud and clear," came their father's response.

Elijah drew a purposeful breath, stowing the camera around his neck. "Okay. Let's press on."

They moved slowly, quietly, around the first corner, observing the footprints, trying hard not to leave too many of their own. It wasn't easy. A huge slab of concrete formed a low bridge ahead of them, a real headbanger. They ducked under it and kept going. There were plenty of spiderwebs spanning the openings and gaps to either side, but so far they hadn't walked into any—another sign that someone had just come through. The darkness was total. The only light was what they'd brought with them.

After ducking, winding, stooping, and almost crawling through a hazardous maze for several yards, they came to another wall with another opening, this one much larger, the size of a doorway. They stopped.

"Smell that?" Elisha asked.

Elijah nodded. A smell of smoke and hot wax, the same odor that fills a room after someone blows out birthday candles. He spoke quietly into his radio, "Mom, Dad, we've reached another wall, with an old doorway. I think this will put us under the new school building."

"We can smell something," Elisha reported, ". . . like candles."

"Stay in touch," said Nate.

They stepped through the doorway into a cavity about twenty feet across. Heaps of broken concrete created a weird, cavelike floor with mounds, dips, towers, and slopes; but they immediately knew they'd arrived. This was it.

On three sides of the room, at least the uppermost half of the original concrete walls was still visible, providing space for weird artwork and gruesome graffiti—horrible faces, gaping wounds, gushing arteries, drooling, suffering, screaming images in bloody reds and sooty blacks. Black iron chains hung on one wall as if to duplicate a medieval dungeon. Two bats—real, but dead—hung by wires from the ceiling.

At one end of the room, against a large, bare wall, was a crude altar: a low table with a black pelt—it looked like it came from a cat—spread upon it. At either end of the table, a half-burned candle stood perched atop a brown beer bottle. Upon the pelt was a brass goblet, and next to the goblet a replica of a human skull. On the wall above the table was an all-too-familiar symbol of a

At one end of the room, against a large, bare wall, was a crude altar: a low table with a black pelt—it looked like it came from a cat—spread upon it.

hanging man with an inscription painted in bold letters underneath: EYRF LEBA.

Elisha put her hand against the wall to steady herself and quickly scanned the room in every direction. Elijah did the same. The beams from their headlamps flew around the room like frantic comets, searching every corner, penetrating every shadow. Neither had to say a word. Each knew the other felt the same fear.

But nothing emerged from the black shadows. Nothing stirred or leaped or screamed. Elisha felt the tips of the candles. They were still warm. Only minutes ago, they'd been burning.

But now, as near as they could tell, they were alone in the room.

With hands still trembling and with constant, furtive glances over his shoulder, Elijah lifted the camera and began taking pictures of the violent artwork, the hanging bats, the chains, and the altar. The flash was as brilliant as lightning in this dark place, burning the images onto Elisha's retinas. When she closed her eyes and looked away, the images were still before her in reversed colors, floating ghostlike in a sea of black, haunting her. It was time to report.

"Mom, Dad—" She had to clear her throat, steady her voice, and start again. "We've found some kind of ritual chamber." She went on to describe it and then added, "And the name Abel Frye is written backward on the wall above the altar." She looked up and described what she saw in the beam of her headlamp. "There's a large heating duct running across the ceiling, and it looks like several large sections of pipe and conduit. I guess that explains how the sound of their voices was carried upstairs into the hallway."

Nate responded, "Any clues as to who these people are?"

She searched around the room as she spoke. "Nothing so far, no articles of clothing or anything like that. The footprints belong to kids, though. That's pretty obvious." She forced herself to look at the artwork again. What Ian Snyder had in his notebook was horrible enough. This was far worse. "From what I see on the walls, we're, uh, we're dealing with some pretty sick people."

⊘⊘

Outside, standing in the hole in the dark, Nate looked up at Tom Gessner and Mr. Loman, who were listening to every word. "Looks like you were right, Mr. Gessner."

Gessner's head sank toward his chest. He was not at all happy to hear that. "Any suggestions?"

Nate spoke into his radio. "Leave everything just the way it is—and do what you can to erase your footprints."

"Okay," Elisha answered. "We're coming out."

Nate looked up at Mr. Gessner and Mr. Loman. "The best way to find out what these people are doing is to observe them doing it, so we'll do our best to pretend we were never here. In the meantime, Mr. Loman, we'd better have another look at Shawna Miller's locker."

⊘⊘

129

The symbol of the hanging man was there, recently etched.

Mr. Loman was flabbergasted. "We *checked* all these lockers!"

"Just after school let out for the day," Nate recalled.

"But the building remained open for a while, right?" Gessner asked.

"Sure," said Mr. Loman. "I don't lock up until about six. Guess whoever did this had time enough while we weren't looking."

"But we could be in great shape here," said Nate, studying the symbol closely. "We've got a locker with a freshly placed hex and a chance to check it out before the victim opens it."

Sarah cautioned, "Meaning we could encounter a booby trap."

"Better us than the victim. At least we're prepared for one."

Mr. Loman had already turned on the lights in the hall where Shawna's locker was located, and Elijah and Elisha added the beams from their headlamps to illuminate the locker. Sarah put on some thick leather gloves while Mr. Loman gently dialed the combination, then, slowly, cautiously, she opened the locker. She checked all around the edges of the opening for any trip wires, devices, intrusions. Nothing seemed out of the ordinary. One by one, she removed the contents, looking for any sign of tampering. Everything looked normal.

"Well," she said, "I guess there's nothing left to do but have a talk with Shawna in the morning. I don't want to go through her personal things without her being here."

"I don't either," said Nate. "Let's stow the gear and go home.

We'll just have to get here early in the morning and have a word with Shawna before she opens this locker."

๛

"You opened my locker?" Shawna Miller, a tall, slender blonde in a cheerleader's outfit, was upset enough just finding Mr. Loman, Tom Gessner, and Sarah waiting by her locker. When they tried to tell her why they'd opened it, she would hardly let them get a word in. "This is *my* locker! It's *my* life! It's *my* privacy!"

"Miss Miller," Sarah began.

"Isn't there something in the law about unreasonable search and seizure? Are you some kind of cop? Let's see your badge."

"No, we're—"

"Then why are you doing this? Is somebody spreading rumors about me or something?"

"No, it's—"

"And now look, everybody's staring at us! They're all thinking—I know what they're thinking, they're thinking this is a drug bust or something. Well, I don't have any drugs in my locker. I don't do drugs and I resent your thinking I do!"

"This isn't a drug bust. We're—"

"Then what are you doing here?"

"We're—"

"Does Ms. Wyrthen know about this? I mean, have you talked to her, Mr. Gessner?"

Sarah tried again. "If I—if I may speak—"

"We're not doing a thing until—"

"Shawna," said Mr. Gessner, "take it easy. Let Mrs. Springfield explain."

Shawna finally slowed to a stop. "So . . . okay, *explain*."

Sarah pointed to the little hanging man in the upper corner of the locker door. "Someone has scratched a hex on your locker. Now, ordinarily, we could probably say, 'So what?' and just call it some weirdo pulling off a little vandalism, but there are four boys in the hospital right now, and you know who they are, and every one of them has the same strange illness, and every one of them had the same mark etched on his locker. Now, we don't know what this illness is or what's causing it, but we do know we don't want the same thing happening to you."

"A hex?" Shawna studied the little symbol closely. Then, suddenly, she smirked. "Abel Frye! Give me a break!"

Sarah prompted her, "So you know something about Abel Frye?"

"Sure, the school ghost, the kid who hanged himself. Everybody's talking about it. But I know who did this. Crystal Sparks. It has to be."

Sarah considered the name. "Crystal Sparks. The girl who painted the picture of Abel Frye?"

Shawna nodded. "She's a witch. She hangs around with that other weirdo, that Ian Snyder. We're always giving them a hard time so they're just trying to get back at us, like they're going to sic their ghost on us." She laughed and said with dripping sarcasm, "Like, oh wow, I'm really scared."

Sarah tried not to appear as fascinated as she was. "So, there's something between you and these—you call them witches?"

"It's no big deal. They're losers, just, just weirdos. Everybody picks on 'em."

"Yourself included?"

Shawna hesitated, shrugged, and finally admitted flippantly, "Yeah."

"So I guess you've made some enemies."

Shawna looked at the little symbol again. "And I don't appreciate them marking up my locker."

"Well, they may have done more than that," said Sarah. "If it's all right with you, we'd better make sure they haven't planted something in your belongings."

"Planted something?" At last, *maybe* Shawna took them seriously. "All right. Go ahead. But if I were you, I'd check *Crystal Sparks'* locker, too!"

"Don't worry, we will. And now, with your permission?"

Shawna opened the locker for them, and stood by with her lower lip sticking out and her arms crossed while Sarah closely examined Shawna's textbooks, a handbag, a jacket, and a cloth bag containing makeup, a hairbrush, a mirror, and a small artist's kit of pastel pencils. Sarah found nothing unusual. She quickly brought in Max, who sniffed the locker and turned away, unimpressed.

"Satisfied?" Shawna asked.

"You wouldn't consider staying away from school for a few days, would you?" Sarah asked.

"No way! I have a perfect attendance record and it's going to stay that way!"

Tom Gessner gave it a try. "Shawna, it's only for your protection."

"Hey," Shawna said, "*I* don't have a problem. If you think there's a problem, then you fix it."

With that, she turned her back on them and headed for her homeroom.

ℰℐ

At lunch period, Elisha was on her way to the lunchroom when she spotted something that didn't look right: Norman Bloom with his back against the wall, fenced in by three big guys who didn't look like they were his friends. As a matter of fact, when Norman tried to leave the discussion, a big walking triangle of a guy shoved him back against the wall and held his hand against Norman's throat. The hallway was busy with lunch-period traffic. Kids were passing by, talking, eating, laughing. Some noticed what was happening, but no one stopped to intervene.

Elisha had no idea what she was going to do—even as she quickened her step.

"Come on, Bloom," one of the big guys was saying, "I'm hungry."

"I don't have money for all of you," Norman replied.

The Triangle put some weight against Norman's throat, and Elisha could tell it hurt. "That's too bad, isn't it? Come *prepared,* Bloom, come *prepared!*"

"Helloooo!" Elisha singsonged, almost skipping up to them. "Norman! I've gotta talk to you!" She said to the others, "Could you excuse us a second?"

Maybe it was her beauty, maybe just the fact that she was a girl, maybe their amazement that a guy like Norman Bloom would even know a girl who looked like her. Whatever the reason, The Triangle let go and he and his buddies backed off. "Sure thing, babe," said one as they all looked her over. Another made a suggestion he should have been ashamed of.

Elisha took Norman by the arm. "Where've you been? I got a call from London today." She led him away quickly, babbling in his ear. "You're never going to guess what she said, Norman! She wants to help with the project, as soon as she gets back. All you have to do is finish framing it up so she can pick out a color."

They got around a corner and Norman asked, "What are you talking about?"

"I don't know, I'm making it up." She stopped and he stopped with her. "What was that all about?"

"What was what all about?"

"John Lassiter, Craig Forbes, and Brock Hanley. They're . . . they're just big muscle guys unsure of their manhood."

"*Duh!* That little meeting back there."

He wouldn't look at her. "They needed some lunch money. It was nothing."

"Nothing? The guy had his hand to your throat!"

His eyes wandered about the hallway. He seemed embarrassed, irritated. "I could have handled it."

"Who were they?"

He went to the side of the hallway to get out of the traffic and she followed. "John Lassiter, Craig Forbes, and Brock Hanley. They're . . . they're just big muscle guys unsure of their manhood."

"Friends of yours?"

He knew her question was only half serious. "No."

"So what were you doing—" She wasn't sure if she should ask. "Norman, were you paying them off?"

That made him mad. "That's none of your business."

"Uh-uh-uh. If somebody's hurting a friend of mine, it's my business."

His eyes were getting wet. She could tell he was in pain and trying not to show it. He looked directly at her and said emphatically, "I do what I have to do to survive. That's how the world works." Then he added, "That's how this school works."

"I don't understand."

"Do I have to spell it out for you?" He looked away, trying to get control. "I'm—I don't have the physical strength or ability to fend these guys off. And they know it. Everybody knows it."

She couldn't believe what she was hearing. "Norman, there

are laws. I mean, they can't just . . . *attack* you. Why don't you tell somebody?"

He laughed bitterly. "Tell who? A teacher? My parents? You think they don't know this stuff is going on?"

"They can't—How could they *allow* it?"

"Oh, kids will be kids, didn't you know that? Everybody gets picked on, it's no big deal, it's just part of growing up. Be a man! No pain! Just buck up and try harder, just ignore them."

"But . . . but that guy *assaulted* you! That's against the law!"

"Tell that to Marquardt!"

"Who's that?"

"The coach. My gym teacher." He pointed toward the scene they'd just left. "Brock Hanley—the guy who had me by the throat?—he's a teaching assistant in fourth period. That's *my* gym class." His pain was giving way to anger. "Marquardt picks the oversized jerks to run things and then looks the other way."

Elisha had to gather herself a moment. "Norman . . . this muscle stuff, this jock stuff . . . let me tell you something. Some of these big athletic guys think they're so cool when they push the brainy guys around, but really, who ends up better off? After the jocks are all hobbling on bad knees and old sports injuries, the nerds and geeks are relaxing in their plush offices in their big techno companies, making lots of money and getting into golf and racquetball. I mean, Bill Gates is crying all the way to the bank, and with your brains, you'll be doing the same thing. You can count on it. Are you listening to me?"

That seemed to cheer him a little. He managed a smile. "You have a way with words, Elisha."

"Well, we're going to do something about this," she responded, fire in her eyes.

☯

When Crystal Sparks arrived in Tom Gessner's office for a little conference, Sarah had to control a snicker, not at Crystal, but at the first thought to go through Sarah's head: *Don't be afrrraid, I only vant a biiiite of your throat!* There wasn't much chance Crystal Sparks could be mistaken for anyone else. She looked like a vampire fresh from her coffin: slinky, dressed in black, with pale complexion, long black hair, and black eye shadow. Sarah felt pity for her. Her weirdness did not fit well; it was just too *intentional*.

"Hi, Crystal," said Tom Gessner. "This is Sarah Springfield. She's a forensic consultant. She's here working on the, uh, well, the Abel Frye situation."

Crystal did not say hello or offer her hand. She only sat down in the chair across from Gessner's desk and stared glumly at them.

Gessner reached toward the shelf and pulled down Crystal's contest-winning painting of Abel Frye. "It's a great painting you did, Crystal. Thanks to you, everybody in school has a very good idea what Abel Frye looks like."

"Thank you," she said. Her first words since she came in.

"I'm curious. This painting is so detailed, so graphic. How did you know what Abel Frye looks like? Did you make this up or is this—"

"He told me what he looks like."

"He speaks to you?" Sarah asked.

Crystal nodded.

"How does he do that exactly?"

"In private. In secret. That's all I can tell you."

Gessner looked at Sarah, her cue to go ahead.

"Crystal," Sarah began, "we're here to find out why some students have been getting sick, and since this all seems to have something to do with Abel Frye, and since you seem to know a lot about him, we were wondering if you could answer a few questions for us."

"It has to happen," she said abruptly.

"What has to happen, Crystal?"

"Justice. Abel Frye died because of injustice, and he knows when the same injustice is done to someone else. Injustice stirs him up, and he strikes. It has to happen."

Sarah nodded. "From what I've seen, he's had reason to strike. There are some kids being treated unfairly at this school."

Crystal didn't say anything. She just nodded slightly.

Sarah had to think a moment before she asked, "We spoke with Shawna Miller this morning." She could see Crystal tense up. "I got the impression that she and her friends have been pretty rough on you. Is that true?"

"We're definitely not friends."

"Do you think Abel Frye would be interested in dealing justice to Shawna Miller?"

"Only Abel Frye would know that."

Tom Gessner said, "We found a hanging-man symbol on Shawna's locker this morning. Could you help us understand what that means?"

Crystal returned their gaze with a steely gaze of her own and replied, "It means that certain decisions have been made and certain forces have been put in motion."

Sarah said, "I'm not sure what you mean."

"It means," Crystal said slowly and cryptically, "that certain persons should be a lot more careful *whom* they torment."

"Certain persons like Shawna Miller?"

Crystal did not respond.

Tom Gessner leaned forward. "Crystal, if there's something between you and Shawna, there are better ways to work things out. You don't have to threaten anybody."

She showed a hint of a smile, as if amused. "It's not my doing. Abel Frye decides."

"But you have a say in it, don't you?"

She only shrugged and replied, "Some things have to happen."

"Just like a search of your locker," Gessner said a little whimsically. Her eyebrows went up. He only returned her own quote to her, "Some things have to happen."

ᘓᘔ

Ian Snyder, in tank top and sweatpants, pulled the rowing bar to his chest, let it return, pulled it, let it return. He had a strong, steady rhythm going. He was making good time on the machine's digital clock.

Elijah stood beside the rowing machine, coaching him along. "Nice and steady now. Keep your legs into it. Chest up, shoulders first, shoulders first. Easy now, you're not racing anybody. This is for you, nobody else."

Baker High School had a nice workout room equipped with weight machines, treadmills, barbells, a rowing machine, the works. Ian Snyder had never been in this room before, at least voluntarily, and Elijah could understand why. Rooms like this could easily become the exclusive territory of the jocks, the athletes, the physically oriented, a place where guys worked their bodies, tried to outdo each other, and carried out seek-and-destroy missions against the physically inferior. The skinny kids, the chubby kids, the just plain nonathletes weren't barred from the place, but most of them quickly learned that any personal program of physical fitness wasn't worth the humiliation.

Elijah and Ian had been talking about that at lunch. They started out talking about self-defense. It turned out Ian was quite impressed with Elijah's skill—and that got them on the subject of physical fitness and how it would be a good thing, even fun, if it weren't such a drag, which got them thinking: Why does it have to be a drag? Can't a guy get some exercise without being made to feel like a wimp?

And then Elijah saw a chance to spend just a little more time with Ian Snyder and get to know him better. "Let's sign up for the rowing machine," he said, all excited.

"Naw . . . ," said Ian.

"Yeah! Come on! You and me! Strength in numbers!"

"Naw . . ."

"Just doing our own thing, going our own speed, just so we can say we did it."

"I've never even used a rowing machine."

That got Elijah even more excited. "Hey! A new experience! I love it!"

So here they were, Ian rowing, Elijah coaching and encouraging, having a great time. And Elijah was able to confirm what he had suspected all along, that Ian Snyder was not nearly as "freaky" as his classmates were so quick to assume. He had a very normal, very human side. He could laugh, he could joke, he could smile and carry on a warm and friendly conversation. All he really needed was a friend, someone who saw right through his weird exterior and cared about the person inside.

"Okay," said Elijah, "one and a half kilometers to go. Gotta get *mean* now, gotta get *hungry!* Pick it up, pick it up, pick it up!"

Ian stepped up his pace, pulling, pulling, pulling, the machine's fan-bladed flywheel spinning up a good breeze, his face filled with a new determination. It was wonderful to see.

Wonderful, but still tough. While Ian was first figuring out the machine, Elijah got several good looks at the soles of his shoes and knew they matched perfectly one set of footprints he'd photographed under the building the previous night. Given all they knew, there could be little doubt that Ian had been there. It wasn't outlandish to think that the voice they had heard and recorded last night belonged to this young man now sweating and rowing his way toward the digital finish line.

So . . . okay, Lord, Elijah kept praying, *what next? Where do we go from here?*

"Hey, angel! What are you doing in here?"

Ian stopped rowing, and the humanness left his face. Elijah turned to see a big guy in running shorts striding toward them. He'd seen this guy before, sauntering around the halls, smirking his way around the lunchroom. This was trouble.

"Come on, angel," he said, motioning for Ian to get off the machine—and he meant "angel" as a smear, not a compliment. "Turn it over."

"We signed up for this machine. It's ours for fifteen more minutes," Elijah said.

The big guy just sneered. "Too bad. It's mine now." He grabbed Ian by the arm. "Off the machine."

Ian jerked his arm free, his face filling with rage.

Now three guys at the pressing bench started watching. "Whoooaaa," they said, "better watch it, Hanley! He's got a ghost working for him, remember?" Obviously, they all thought that was very funny.

Elijah stepped up, his head coming to the level of the big guy's chest. "Hey. There are rules. There are policies. We signed in fair and square. You have to wait your turn."

The big guy's friends were watching. He grabbed two fistfuls of Elijah's tee shirt and lifted Elijah off his feet. "What did you say?"

Well, thought Elijah, *all he can do is kill me.* "I said—"

"HEY!" There was no mistaking the gruff, gravelly roar of Mr. Marquardt. He was striding their way, every eye in the place upon him, whistle around his neck, clipboard in hand.

The big guy set Elijah down and Elijah straightened out his shirt as he thought, *All right, now we'll get some justice around here.*

"Snyder," Marquardt hollered, "get off that machine!"

Ian got up.

"Thanks, freak," said the big guy, taking over.

"But we reserved the rowing machine for half an hour!" Elijah protested.

Marquardt gave no indication of hearing him. "Okay, Hanley, five kilometers, starting now!" He started a stopwatch. Hanley started rowing. "Looking good, looking good."

Ian brushed past Elijah. "Let's go."

Elijah approached to Mr. Marquardt. "Excuse me, Mr. Marquardt—"

"I am *busy!*" Marquardt roared in his face. *"Get out of here!"*

It took a moment for Elijah to accept that there was nothing more he could do or say. Marquardt, Hanley, and the three guys on the pressing bench owned this little club; and he and Ian were out, policy or no policy, sign-up sheet or no sign-up sheet.

By the time he joined Ian on the sidewalk outside, he was furious. "I don't believe this!"

Ian had his old steely gaze back, but was much calmer, as if resigned to it. "I saw it coming."

"We signed up. Marquardt had the sign-up sheet right on his desk! I know because I put it there!"

"His athletes get priority."

"That's not what the rules say!"

"Welcome to Baker High."

Elijah was genuinely angry. "Would you please explain this to me?"

Ian thought a moment, then gave a little shrug. "There are two Baker High Schools. There's the one everybody *wants* to see—the one with the rules and the policies and the cool principal walking around in her business suits and all the happy students in their name-brand clothes. It's got the honor roll and the trophies in the display case, the honor students and the athletes get their pictures in the paper, and nothing bad ever happens, and look! We have metal detectors, the first in the county!

"And then . . . there's you and me standing out here while certain people do whatever they want at our expense. They set up their own little club, decide who gets in, then dump on everybody else. They spit on 'em, push 'em around, trip 'em, slap 'em, steal their clothes and their money, grab 'em where they shouldn't be grabbed. The teachers have the power to do something about it but don't, and the parents . . . well, they just make us come here every day, that's all. That's the other Baker High."

Elijah was trying to think clearly and objectively about all this. Not everyone at Baker was as Ian had described, but still, all he could see was Hanley lifting him off his feet—*assaulting* him— and Marquardt not doing a thing about it. "If I found out *my* kid was being treated this way, I'd sure do something about it."

"Well, *my* parents—" He stopped right there. Then he said, "Well, sometimes you just have to take care of yourself, Elijah. Nobody's going to do it for you."

Elijah had no answer.

"What would you like to see done to that guy?"

Elijah looked at those cold, dark eyes. "Who?"

"Marquardt. What would you like to see happen to him?"

That tipped Elijah just a little off balance. Was Ian really going to invite him into the darker side of his life? Elijah kept his own anger out of it when he asked, "What did you have in mind?"

Ian drew a long breath, then just leaned back and smiled. "Oh . . . something."

7

AMY AND CRYSTAL

Julia Baynes, Leonard Baynes' mother, was hardly presentable when Nate, Sarah, and Tom Gessner knocked on her door. She hadn't had a shower, she reeked of cigarette smoke, and years of alcohol had noticeably dampened her wits. The fact that she had no husband did not help matters any, and now, to top it all off, her son was in critical condition in the hospital.

"Hello, Mrs. Baynes," said Gessner. "You remember Nate Springfield?"

She stared at Nate blankly.

"From the hospital?" Gessner prompted.

It registered. "Oh! Yeah! Hi."

"This is his wife, Sarah."

"Hi." She shook Sarah's hand, then looked at Gessner. "So, what's up?"

Gessner spoke gently. "We made an appointment, remember? To see Leonard's room?"

"Yeah, right. Come in." She stood aside, hardly looking at them.

"Thank you so much, Mrs. Baynes," said Sarah. "We'll try not to be long."

Nate had Mr. Maxwell at his side. "Do you mind if our dog comes in to help us search?"

She shrugged, lighting another cigarette. "I like dogs. Take all the time you need."

"Could you show us Leonard's room?" Nate asked.

She drew a breath through the cigarette and the smoke came out her mouth as she said, "This way."

They passed through the small, messy living room, stepping through old magazines and junk mail that littered the worn carpet, and down a narrow hall. Leonard's room was at the end.

"Sorry for the mess," Mrs. Baynes said.

"It's quite all right," said Sarah, surveying the cramped, cluttered bedroom. "Are any of Leonard's—" When she turned, Mrs. Baynes was walking away from them, up the hall. "Uh, Mrs. Baynes?"

Mrs. Baynes hesitated as if someone may have called her name. "Huh?"

"Are any of Leonard's things—you know, coats, hats, things he takes to school—would they be anywhere else in the house besides here in his room?"

She said, "I dunno," and shuffled around the corner into the kitchen.

"I'll see what I can find out," said Gessner, going up the hall to speak with Mrs. Baynes.

Nate and Sarah exchanged a knowing look, then slipped on some surgical gloves and turned to the task at hand.

"Okay, Max," Nate said.

Max started sniffing around the room, going along the floor, poking his nose under the bed, sniffing the dresser.

The room was a mess, with clothes scattered everywhere. It would take a while to sort through it all—as if they had "a while." As far as they were concerned, Shawna Miller was next. But her parents were very proud of her perfect attendance record and didn't want it jeopardized. With Shawna's careless attitude, there wasn't much they could do to keep "it" from happening to her.

As for Crystal Sparks, she was absent from school today and couldn't be found at home either, so they couldn't question her further. The search through her locker told them she was into black, slithery clothing, dark makeup, and weird art, but that was all they learned about her—except for a certain scent Max found. Again, he didn't alert as if he'd found drugs, but he was keenly interested in whatever it was.

They found nothing in Leonard's locker, and Max didn't smell anything of interest either, so now they were searching his room, combing through his socks, shirts, pants, and underwear, scattered CDs, half-broken model cars, and heavy-metal magazines in the hope of finding out what had happened to him and the others.

While Nate started going through the closet and Max just kept sniffing everywhere, Sarah went through Leonard's dresser. Every article of clothing was wadded up and mixed in with all the others, and there seemed to be more useless junk in the drawers than clothing. There were some dirty magazines buried in the bottom drawer. She left them there. Atop the dresser was an old photograph of Leonard, his older sister, and both parents. They had been a family at one time. No doubt, Leonard missed those days.

Nate found a well-worn army surplus jacket in the closet. A vest pocket contained a crumpled sheet of notebook paper, a recent quiz in U.S. government. Leonard got a D. Nate began checking the other pockets. He found a pair of sunglasses in one pocket, a set of keys and some change in another, an old, half-eaten candy bar still in the wrapper in a third, and along with that—

A soda straw.

"Sarah . . ."

She received it from his hand and examined it, looking down one end and then the other. "Looks like some sugar crystals inside." She sniffed it. "Same as the other one. I'd say we have a pattern here."

"Max . . ."

Max had found the old army coat and now he was craning his neck, sniffing it up and down with that same captivated look in his eyes.

What is *he smelling?* Sarah wondered.

☙

Back in the Holy Roller, she scraped samplings from inside the straw, put the samples into a row of test tubes, and quickly ascertained the same things she found in the previous straw.

"Sugar, but with another chemical mixed in. My second screening indicated a petroleum base, so it isn't LSD, cocaine, or meth. I sent a sample back to the university to see if they could figure out what it is. But look here."

Nate leaned over her shoulder to take a close look at what she was showing him.

"See these stains? The sugar seems to have been concentrated in two small areas." She pointed them out with the tip of her tweezers. "Right here, about two inches from the end, and then here, about two inches from the other end. It's as if the sugar formed two small plugs at one time, blocking the straw in two places."

Nate straightened and thought a moment. "So, if we play 'what if . . .' What if these straws are some kind of drug-making or drug-taking device?"

"If they are, it's brand-new. I've never seen anything like it before." She sighed in frustration. "I wish these victims weren't out of their minds. I'd like to ask them about this."

"What if they don't know anything anyway? What if Ian Snyder and his friends are behind this? They could have planted a straw in Tod Kramer's duffel bag and Leonard Baynes' pocket."

"They could plant a straw just about anywhere—in desks, backpacks, coats, lockers . . ."

"But what in the world do the straws do, and how do they do it?" Nate drummed his fingers on his chin. "Then again, Ian Snyder and his friends may have nothing to do with it at all. This could be something totally unrelated."

"Well . . . Elijah says he might be getting close to something."

"In the meantime, we'd better find out everything there is to know about this straw."

The next day, during biology class, Elisha volunteered to gather up plant cuttings from the other students and put them all in rooting mix back in the supply room—where Norman happened to be working at the time.

He was glad to see her, and eagerly helped her measure out the correct proportions of ingredients for the rooting mix. "Two and half peat moss, two and a half vermiculite, three sand . . ."

"Norman," she ventured as she scooped out the right amount of sand, "I've been meaning to ask you about all this Abel Frye stuff."

He sniffed a little chuckle and spoke as he worked. "Abel Frye, the patron saint of the geeks and the nerds, the weird and the weak."

"What do you mean?"

"Well, according to the big legend going around, Abel Frye was a smart kid with plenty of potential, but he was weak and he was different, so the bullies trounced on him. They made his life so miserable that he finally hanged himself. That sort of makes him the patron saint of the nerds, the geeks, the little people: the weak and the weird." Then he added, "You know, people like me."

"Norman. You're not weird. You *are* different, but I see that as a quality and not a fault."

"Aren't you going to tell me I'm not weak?"

That flustered her a little. "Norman . . . everybody's weaker than somebody!"

He sighed, and then he smiled. "And not everybody who's strong is a bully, either. I've tried to keep that in mind. But to answer your question, think about this: Everybody who's gotten sick and gone crazy *was* a bully who picked on Ian Snyder. Jim Boltz and his three friends all used to pick on him, and Leonard Baynes, man, that was obvious. So it's a no-brainer: Ian Snyder's the one to watch."

She was careful to keep her voice down as she said, "I've heard a lot of kids say he's controlling the ghost."

That made him laugh, although he tried to laugh quietly. "Well, sure. He wants everyone to think that. It's his way of fighting back—and it's working. I think a lot of victims are starting to look up to him."

"Victims?"

"Well, other kids who get picked on."

"Like Crystal Sparks, maybe?"

He thought a moment. "You'll know who she is the moment you see her. She's like an Ian Snyder clone. But that's just it: These other kids think Abel Frye's going to stick up for them, too, and since Ian controls Abel Frye, they start hanging around with him, joining up with the weird outcasts. It's a little group all their own, all of them weird. But this ghost stuff is all hysteria. Some of the kids are so into it that they start thinking they're really seeing and hearing something."

"So what really happened to the guys in the hospital?"

He thought a moment, quite seriously. "That part's real, but I haven't a clue what's doing it. I just don't think it's a ghost. The kids are all adding that part to it. They're blaming it on Abel Frye—which suits Ian Snyder just fine. Whatever's causing this sickness, he's taking big advantage of it."

"So is he really a witch?"

Norman was serious when he said, "He and his friends are

into some pretty strange things. And if I can be honest, I think your brother better be careful."

ॐ

At lunch, Elijah sat down across the table from Ian, a surefire way to draw stares from around the lunchroom.

Ian was impressed. "You've got a lot of nerve sitting here."

Elijah glanced around. Ian was right. Others in the lunchroom were giving him the curious and judgmental eye. Even his buddies from calculus class were staring at him and talking between themselves in hushed, gossipy tones.

Ian had become quite the topic of conversation around the classrooms and hallways. Those with reason to fear him were finally beginning to fear him, and a new group of outcasts—some weak, some weird, all of them on the fringe—were starting to occupy the lunch stools at Ian's table. He was both feared and admired, and obviously enjoying it.

Well, Elijah thought, bravely meeting the eyes looking his way, *they'll just have to go on staring and talking.* He spoke to Ian in a quiet voice. "I've been thinking about what you said about Marquardt."

That got the attention of an earringed, orange-haired sophomore two chairs away and a plain-looking fat kid sitting beside Elijah. They leaned in, chewing their lunches, ready to listen.

Ian only smiled and took another bite from his sandwich. His mouth was a little full when he said, "How bad do you want it to happen?"

Elijah studied Ian's face. This was going to be a delicate balancing act: asking questions, but not too many, and only the kind of questions that Ian would be comfortable answering. "You told me—remember when we were having that big old incident with Leonard Baynes?"

Ian answered proudly, looking not only at Elijah but at his new followers, "I said Leonard Baynes would be dealt with." Then he sat quietly, letting what happened to Leonard Baynes speak for itself.

Elijah asked very hesitantly, "Did you . . . I mean, can you really do that?"

Ian didn't seem angry when he said, "Be careful you don't ask too many questions."

Elijah shrank back just a little. "Yeah. Right."

But Ian volunteered, "The same thing that happened to Baynes can happen to Marquardt—and Hanley. Don't ask me how. It just can."

Elijah dared to push just a little further. "But what about those other guys? You know, Tod Kramer, and Doug Anderson, and, uh . . ."

"Jim Boltz."

"Yeah."

Ian had a wicked glint in his eye. "Like I said, Elijah: You have to take care of yourself. Nobody's going to do it for you. It's like—"

A crash! Screams. Dishes flew off a table. A lunch stool toppled and tumbled along the floor. Every head turned.

Two rows away a pretty brown-haired girl had leaped to her feet, her hands extended and clawing like a cat as if fending off an attacker, her eyes wild with terror. "No, no, don't am makin' badder, I can't, I can't!"

"All right . . . ," said the orange-haired sophomore.

The girl lurched backward, tripping and falling into the people seated at a table behind her. They reached out to catch her and she fought them, screaming, kicking, and thrashing as if for her life. She grabbed up a lunch stool and tried to throw it.

The fat kid beside Elijah looked troubled. "But . . . but that's Amy! She's not—"

Amy's friends surrounded her, grabbed the stool, tried to subdue her. A teacher came running. Her friends held her by her arms as she fought them, staring straight ahead at *something*. "No, no, been waving far away, never, no . . ." Then she said something that caught every ear in the place. "No, Abel Frye! No!"

> The girl lurched backward, tripping and falling into the people seated at a table behind her. They reached out to catch her and she fought them, screaming, kicking, and thrashing as if for her life. She grabbed up a lunch stool and tried to throw it.

A whisper rippled and ricocheted around the room. "Abel Frye!" "It's the ghost!" "It's Abel Frye!"

"Go, Abel!" said Orange Hair.

Amy screamed all the louder, "Abel, leave me alone!"

That brought screams of terror from some of the other girls. Some of the kids actually ducked behind their tables as if they could hide from this *thing*, whatever it was.

"Ian . . ." The fat kid's voice sounded pleading.

Elijah was as captured by the sight as anyone, but then he heard a clamor behind him and looked to see Ian Snyder on his feet, horrified. "No," Ian was muttering, "no, not her. Not her!"

Elijah was mystified. "Ian?"

Ian was looking toward the screaming, struggling girl, now being carried out by her friends and two teachers. "Leave her alone. *Stop* it!"

They carried Amy out of the room, but her screams continued to echo down the hallway and into the lunchroom. Every eye was locked on the doorway. Some students couldn't bear the sound and covered their ears.

Ian sank into his chair, visibly troubled, his fingers over his mouth.

The screaming faded with distance, and then a faraway door—probably the nurse's office—slammed shut.

Commotion and weird, fearful confusion broke out all across the lunchroom. The kids were looking at each other, hiding behind each other, chattering, whispering, crying. A few smirked and mocked, but only a few. Mrs. Donaldson, the English teacher, moved through the room. "All right, everyone, now just calm down. She's going to be all right. Just calm down."

Suddenly, Sherri Cook, a junior, an attractive red-haired cheerleader, ran down the aisle between the tables and knelt beside Ian, shaking, tears in her eyes. "Ian! Ian, if you're doing this, please make it stop! Amy's my friend! She's a good person; she never hurt anybody!"

But Ian only sat there looking dumbfounded. This was something Elijah had never seen before: Ian Snyder at a total loss. "I didn't—"

Now Mike Hagan came over, a nice guy Elijah knew from English class. "Ian. Let's talk. We can work this out."

Ian got to his feet, Sherri and Mike on either side, still trying to reason with him. He did not look cool, sinister, or defiant. He looked scared.

Elijah got up as well, not knowing what to say or do.

"Come on," said Mike. "Whatever the problem is, we'll work it out. Just—just call it off."

"Please!" said Sherri.

Everyone in the room was staring at them—even some of the big jocks. Even Shawna Miller.

Ian turned, pushed his way past Mike and Sherri, and strode —or maybe *fled*—through the outside exit door.

The room exploded in fearful, rapid chatter. "*He's* doing this?" "Don't you get it? He controls the ghost!" "Yeah, *right!*" "Well, she must have done *something* to make him mad!" "She's OD'd on something, that's all." "I hear the feds are after him."

The fat kid and Orange Hair just sat there dumbfounded, but Elijah ran after Ian, flinging the exit door open and dashing through, heeling to a halt on the sidewalk outside and frantically looking all directions. *Oh man, which way?* Ian could have gone straight across the parking lot. He could have ducked into the woods. He could have disappeared around one of three different corners.

Whichever direction he chose, he was gone.

೧೦

Not wasting a second, not saying a word, Nate ran into the lunchroom and gathered up Amy Warren's schoolbooks and carry bag. Officer Carrillo wasted no time either, immediately putting up a yellow tape barrier around Amy's locker. Mr. Loman brought the combination, and Nate and Sarah, thick gloves protecting their hands, opened it. Only one thing inside appeared unusual: a duffel bag, the kind the football players carried. The owner's name was printed on the side in black marker: Jim Boltz.

೧೦

"She's Jim Boltz's girlfriend," Tom Gessner explained. "As near as I've been able to gather from their friends, she took the duffel bag off the players' bench that night when Jim got sick. She was keeping it for him and had no idea we were looking for it."

Gessner, Officer Carrillo, Nate, and Sarah were meeting behind closed doors with Ms. Wyrthen. Everyone was feeling the tension, the horror, the helplessness; and tempers were approaching the flash point.

Officer Carrillo was checking his gun for the umpteenth time, rotating the cylinder, checking every chamber for a bullet.

"Officer Carrillo," said Ms. Wyrthen, "I'd feel so much better if you'd put that thing away."

"Something's out there," he replied, "and whatever it is, it's going to be sorry it ever ran into me."

"I think it's time we considered closing the school down," Gessner suggested.

"I've already looked into that," said Ms. Wyrthen. "Unless there's a real emergency, I can't suspend classes without a two-thirds approval from the school board."

"So?" Carrillo demanded. "Get approval!"

"Show me an emergency!" she countered. "Give me a fire, an earthquake, asbestos in the ceiling panels. The school board will understand those, but *this*? What is it? What are we really dealing with? I can't tell them we're haunted by a ghost!"

"But there's something out there!"

"Dan . . ." Tom Gessner tried to calm him. "The gun?"

Carrillo grudgingly holstered his weapon. "Well, at least close off the Forbidden Hallway!"

Sarah countered, "We don't have a conclusive pattern to show that hallway has anything to do with this."

Carrillo was insulted and all the more angry. "Well what *do* you have? That's what I want to know!"

Ms. Wyrthen turned to Nate and Sarah. "What have you found?"

Nate reported first. "We cleared Amy's locker and we have the entire contents sealed up for examination. Our dog sniffed the locker and the contents, and we think he's found something. We just don't know what it is."

"You don't know?" Carrillo practically yelled. "Would you mind explaining that?"

Nate responded calmly, "Max is trained to find illicit drugs *or* any other scent we can isolate and teach him. The problem is, we have to know what we're looking for so we can give him the scent to sniff for. Right now, it's working in reverse: Max is starting to notice a scent that alerts him, but we'll have to go through a trial-and-error process to identify it."

"We're going to go through all of Amy's things, down to the smallest item, until we find it," said Sarah. "But note this as well: We went through Crystal Sparks' locker and Max found the same scent, whatever it is. We didn't find anything that would tie her to the victims, just her school things, some outer clothing, and some more of her weird paintings, but Max is finding some kind of connection with his nose."

Carrillo growled, "Well, I say we haul in this Snyder kid and this Sparks chick and get it out of them."

"But they have rights!" Ms. Wyrthen reminded the officer.

"I'll read them their rights!" Carrillo snapped back. Then he pointed his finger in Nate's face. "But I'll get results, which is a lot more than we've gotten from you!"

Nate put up his hand to signal for caution. "We're getting real close to hearing from Ian Snyder, don't worry. But I'm troubled about something: Amy Warren's locker doesn't have a hex scratched on it, that hanging-man symbol."

"So what? She got hauled screaming to the hospital, isn't that enough?"

"It's a lot. But it isn't everything, and I'll venture it's not enough to detain Ian Snyder."

It was Sarah's turn. She spoke quietly but quickly. "Consistent with the pattern, we found a soda straw in Jim Boltz's duffel bag, identical to the other two."

That got a visible reaction.

She continued, "We checked all three straws for fingerprints, but no results. However, they all had two things in common: small deposits of sugar that seem to indicate the straws were once plugged with sugar at both ends, and a chemical that up until now we couldn't identify." She unfolded a sheet of paper. "But we just got this fax from an associate at the university. The sugar was saturated with a chemical trade-named Tricanol."

"Tricanol?" Officer Carrillo repeated.

"It's an additive used in paints, stains, wood preservatives. It's used widely and it's widely available."

Ms. Wyrthen wrinkled her nose. *"Paint?"*

"Does it produce the symptoms we've seen?" Gessner asked.

Sarah sighed and folded the paper. "Afraid not. It can be poisonous in large amounts, but it isn't hallucinogenic or neurotoxic. All that is to say, it probably has no direct relation to the sickness—but it has to mean something. It's a clue and we have to track it down."

Ms. Wyrthen forced a pleasant, professional smile. "So I

would say we're making progress." She made a point to look at Carrillo. "Slow, perhaps, but progress nevertheless."

"Progress?" said Carrillo. "Some wood preservative is progress?"

The telephone on Ms. Wyrthen's desk chirped. "Excuse me. This could be important." She picked up the phone. "Ms. Wyrthen."

"We'll check the wood shop, first of all," said Nate.

"I'll get the students' class schedules and we'll see who's been through that room lately," Gessner offered.

"And maybe we'll check the greenhouse as well," Sarah offered. "The shelves in the greenhouse are probably treated with preservative."

"Right," said Nate, "and then . . ." His voice trailed off. He was looking at Ms. Wyrthen.

Her face was pale as she sank into her chair. The others read her expression and fell silent. She picked up her pen. Her hand was trembling. "Do you have the mother's name and number?" She listened, and wrote it down. "And the medical examiner? Okay." She wrote some more. "Okay. I'll tell the others. Thank you. Call if you get anything else." She hung up.

Everyone was waiting.

Nate asked, "What is it, Ms. Wyrthen?"

She looked up at them, her face pale and troubled. "That was Dr. Stuart at the hospital. Amy Warren . . . is dead. She passed away in the hospital only minutes ago."

Stunned silence. Tom Gessner sank into a chair, resting his head in his hand. Carrillo, red-faced with anger, hooked his thumb through his belt—near his revolver.

After swallowing the initial shock, Nate looked at Sarah. They were each thinking the same thing.

"Its properties have changed," said Sarah. "It's become more lethal."

Nate nodded. "The other victims are still alive after close to two weeks. Amy died within hours."

As Ms. Wyrthen picked up the phone to make a call, Carrillo gave Nate a cold, demanding glare. "So what's next, Springfield? I'd love to hear what your next move is going to be."

He thought for only a moment, then nodded resignedly to himself. "Same procedure. Go through Amy's things, visit her home. But I'll hand you one thing: Looks like we'll have to press a little harder for a talk with Ian Snyder."

"And *another* talk with Crystal Sparks," Sarah offered. "Allegedly, she's one of the witches, one of Ian Snyder's friends, and I know she's holding back plenty."

"That won't be possible," said Ms. Wyrthen, hanging up the phone, her hand trembling. "I just spoke with the medical examiner. The police have found Crystal Sparks. She was . . . her mother said she went raving mad last night and ran out of the house. That's why she wasn't in school today. The police didn't find her until an hour ago—in Benton Park."

"She spent the whole night in Benton Park?" Carrillo asked.

Ms. Wyrthen looked at them directly. "She *died* in Benton Park. The medical examiner guesses she's been dead since last night. We've lost her, too."

8

HANGMAN'S CURSE

T HE NEXT MORNING, there had been no closure notice and classes were in session as usual. More than fifty students stayed home anyway. Shawna Miller was staying home with full permission and parental supervision. Other parents were calling the school office and tying up the telephone. Doctors and cops were coming and going. Local newspaper, radio, and television reporters were popping up in front of the school and in the halls, shoving microphones in students' and teachers' faces.

Word was spreading quickly all over the school: Amy Warren was dead. Crystal Sparks was dead. Tod Kramer was near death. Doug Anderson and Jim Boltz were critical. Leonard Baynes was crazy and getting worse.

As for the mysterious hanging-man symbol, everyone knew about it. It was impossible to keep the lockers of the victims off-limits. Plenty of students were checking their own lockers to make sure they weren't next.

Rumors were popping up out of nowhere and flying at light speed: The next victim was already chosen and it would be a girl; it would be another guy; it would be a friend of the first three; it would be a teacher. Abel Frye was seen in the Forbidden

Hallway; he was seen in the parking lot; he was seen on the roof of the school. Ian Snyder was dead; Ian Snyder had been arrested; Ian Snyder hanged himself. Crystal Sparks hanged herself.

ೲ

"Now, *please* tell me we have an emergency!" Nate protested as he and Sarah met privately with Tom Gessner and Ms. Wyrthen.

"The school board is 'undecided,'" Ms. Wyrthen lamented.

"*Undecided?*" Tom Gessner marveled.

"I didn't hear that," said Sarah. "I *couldn't* have heard that."

"Oh, brother." Gessner wilted at a thought. "It's the game, isn't it?"

Ms. Wyrthen gave a furtive nod. "The championship on Thanksgiving Day. I know at least two board members who have kids on the team and don't want us to forfeit that game, and we'd definitely forfeit if we closed the school." She sighed. "They've told me to wait until they decide for sure."

"And how long will that take?" Nate asked.

"I'm sure we will have enjoyed our turkey and cranberries before then." They all deflated with a moan. "We'll try to cut back on whatever activities we can. The main thing now is to remain calm and keep the students calm, and please, let's try to put a lid on all this hysteria and all these silly rumors. They're only making things worse."

Nate regathered himself and said, "So, I guess we'd better have that talk with Ian Snyder."

"Ian Snyder is missing," said Ms. Wyrthen.

"*What?*"

"Not good, not good," said Gessner.

"Officer Carrillo tried to bring him in for questioning last night—" said Ms. Wyrthen.

Nate and Sarah leaned forward.

"He didn't!" said Nate.

"Please say you're joking," said Sarah.

Ms. Wyrthen put up her hand. "He got no farther than the front door of Ian's house. Ian's mother wouldn't let him in and he didn't have a warrant."

Nate drew a breath. "So now Ian could be anywhere—except here where we can find him."

"Carrillo's prowling the halls right now," Sarah recalled. "He's probably still on the hunt. This doesn't help us. Not at all."

"*Whew!* We need to pray."

"I'll join you," said Gessner.

"Ms. Wyrthen, it's your office. Do you mind if we have a word of prayer?"

"As principal of this school," she said, "I insist on it."

ॐ

When Elijah opened his locker, he found a possible answer to their prayers: a crumpled note from Ian Snyder, jammed through the ventilation slots.

ॐ

"I don't know what to do," Ian said, sitting with his wrists around his knees, hardly looking up.

Elijah and Ian were perched on a cold metal catwalk in the dark recesses above the stage in the main auditorium. From where they sat, they could look down on the racks of stage lights, touch the heavy stage rigging, see the stage floor far below. The towering, vertical curtains below them made them feel they were clinging to a ledge on the side of a skyscraper.

Elijah was skipping Mr. Carlson's humanities class to have this meeting. He was hoping his dad could work it out later with the powers that were.

Ian was hiding, and not just from Carrillo. He kept his voice down. "The others want to know what went wrong. They want me to stop it from happening."

Elijah knew he would have to be somewhat bold. It was definitely time for answers. "Well . . . just what *is* happening, Ian?"

Ian looked up at him, his pale, ghostly face half visible in the dark. "You're a Christian, so you're probably not going to like this, but . . . Elijah, I'm a witch. I have special powers. I have spirits that work for me. You're into spiritual things. Maybe you can believe that."

Elijah knew Ian could be tampering with spirits—*or* this whole problem could have another cause they had yet to discover. For now, he would see it Ian's way. "Is Abel Frye one of the spirits?"

Ian hesitated a moment, but finally nodded.

Elijah considered that a moment and then answered, "I guess he *used* to work for you. Looks like now he's doing stuff on his own, am I right?"

Ian's eyes were fearful. "I never told him to hit Amy. Amy's a friend. Out of all the kids in school, she was one person who actually said 'hi' to me once in a while. She never hurt me, she never shoved me, she never insulted me or talked about me behind my back. She even got on Jim's case for what he was doing to me." He was near tears. "It was supposed to be Shawna Miller. I told him to go after Shawna Miller, not Amy."

The chanting of the other night, Elijah thought.

Ian's head dropped and he shook it slowly in remorse. "And I sure didn't put any curse on Crystal."

"Crystal was a friend, too, right?"

"More than that."

"Was she a witch?"

"I can't get into that." He looked up, not at Elijah but into the darkness surrounding them. "But I'm in trouble. The others are mad. They're ready to kill me. They're blaming me for what happened."

"What others? Who do you mean? Those guys at lunch yesterday?"

"No, those guys are just, you know, new friends. They're not on the inside."

"The inside? Like an inner-circle kind of thing?"

Ian gave in. "There are other witches. But it's a secret group. I can't tell you who they are."

"But they think you put a curse on Amy and Crystal?"

"They think I've lost control of the ghost. And maybe I have. I mean, it was working! I put a curse on Tod Kramer, and *bam!* Abel got him. I put a curse on Doug Anderson, and *bam!* Abel got him, too. Same with Jim Boltz, and same with Leonard Baynes."

"That's a pretty good record."

"Yeah, up until now. Only missed once before, but that time *nothing* happened. Abel didn't hit somebody else."

Elijah prayed he'd get a straight answer as he asked, "You mean, you put a curse on somebody and it didn't work?"

"Can't say for sure. It might still happen."

"Was it Mr. Marquardt?"

Ian seemed to regret his answer. "No. Somebody else. I haven't had a chance to curse Marquardt yet. But I could do it—I mean, I *used* to be able to do it." He smiled. "It was great, Elijah. Everybody who ever tortured me, I could get back at them. I could just . . . *remove* them." He looked at Elijah, strangely gleeful even in his pain. "It's a lot better than guns. Guns are a stupid idea. You try to get your enemies with guns, you just end up getting killed yourself, or thrown in jail—and now with the metal detectors . . ." He chuckled at that. "But nobody can stop a curse. It can go through walls and doors and metal detectors and nobody can turn it away. It's perfect."

"But what do you—I mean, how do you get Abel Frye to go after somebody?"

"Oh, you have a séance and you call him up, you chant your enemy's name several times, you give the ghost an offering, and away he goes."

He makes it sound so simple, Elijah thought. He could only imagine what kind of weird, dark ceremonies Ian and his cohorts must have carried on in their eerie hiding place under the school building. "You, uh, you put the little symbol on the lockers?"

"Me or one of the others. It's supposed to guide the ghost to the right person."

"And then what, you put something in the lockers?"

"What do you mean?"

"Well, you know, some object or something to tag the person. I thought witches did that."

Ian considered that. "Maybe that's what we did wrong. Maybe the little symbol wasn't enough. We should have stuck something in the lockers to keep the curse focused."

Elijah wasn't expecting this kind of answer. "So you didn't, you know, plant anything in their pockets, or in their duffel bags?"

Ian seemed perplexed. "No. I never thought of that."

And now Elijah had to think for a moment. "Well, Ian, if I may speak freely here . . ."

"Go ahead."

"How do you even know you're in contact with a ghost? How do you know this isn't all a weird coincidence?"

He smirked a bit. "Some coincidence. I put out curses and people end up in the hospital."

"Or worse," Elijah reminded him.

Ian admitted, "Yeah, a lot worse."

"You've got a strong case, I'll give you that. So how do you know the ghost's name?"

"He told us his name."

"He talks to you?"

Ian grimaced as if he'd heard a stupid question. "We used a Ouija board."

Elijah got the picture. "Oh. So he spelled it out."

"Sure."

"Ian, how do you know you were really controlling the ghost in the first place? How do you know it wasn't controlling you, just setting you up?"

Ian was silent. He didn't have a comeback for that one.

"I'm not here to preach to you, but yeah, I'm a Christian. I believe in God, and Jesus is my Savior, so let me just give it to you straight: The Bible says a lot about dabbling in witchcraft and messing around with spirits. You never really control the craft or the spirits, Ian. They control you, and they can make a real mess of your life. If there is a spirit involved, I don't think you lost control of it. You never had control in the first place. If you did, we wouldn't be sitting here right now." Elijah let that sink in, and then added, "And you know what? As long as you carry hatred and revenge in your heart, they're going to go right on controlling you. You're never going to be truly free. There's a better way, Ian."

Ian didn't appear to need much convincing of that.

ॐ

Elijah was hoping he could conceal himself in the hasty, between-classes crowd, but Mr. Carlson nabbed him anyway, right out in the middle of the hall. "Well, well, Mr. Springfield! And there you were, telling me there's a right and a wrong. What's your moral judgment on skipping classes?"

Elijah didn't even have time to answer before another voice

intervened. "Excuse me, Mr. Carlson." It was Elijah's dad, dressed like a custodian and looking rather stern. "Am I to understand he skipped your class?"

Carlson gladly reported, "He most certainly did."

Nate took Elijah's arm with a stern expression on his face. "If you don't mind, I'd like to deal with him first."

Mr. Carlson seemed to savor the idea that Elijah was in double trouble. "Well, certainly. When you're finished with him, send him my way."

"Thank you," said Nate, taking Elijah by the arm. "Come on, son, let's have ourselves a little talk."

They hurried down the hall, around a corner, and through a door near the school office.

It was a conference room. Sarah and Elisha were already there.

Elijah waited for the door to close behind him, then reported in a hushed, urgent voice, "Ian didn't plant those soda straws. He didn't plant anything. He summoned up the ghost, and he or one of the other witches scratched the symbol on the locker, but that was all."

Nate, Sarah, and Elisha all exchanged looks.

"What about Amy Warren and Crystal Sparks?" Nate asked.

"He had nothing to do with that. They weren't his enemies, and Crystal Sparks was actually a friend. He says the ghost hit them without being asked to. He's afraid he's lost control."

Nate concluded, "He was never in control of any ghost in the first place."

"This is no ghost," Sarah agreed. "There's a visible, tangible method here. These victims are being set up by human hands."

"It's just like Norman said," Elisha ventured. "Ian isn't the cause of this at all. Something else—or some*one* else—is, and he just *thinks* he is."

"Pretty incredible coincidence, though," said Sarah.

"Well, how incredible? What's his track record?" Nate asked, pulling out his pen and pad and sitting at the conference table.

"He's taking credit for the first four victims," said Elijah. "He told the ghost to strike Tod Kramer, Doug Anderson, Jim Boltz, and Leonard Baynes, and they got hit with . . . whatever it is. But he did say there was another one he cursed, but nothing happened."

"Shawna Miller," said Sarah.

"No, no, he cursed Shawna Miller, but the curse landed on Amy instead."

"This is too weird," Elisha lamented.

"So which curse landed on Crystal?" Sarah asked.

"There wasn't one. That one just happened."

"Okay, so there's one . . . 'curse' . . . still floating around that hasn't landed yet?" Nate asked, his pen poised above his paper. "Who's the intended victim?"

"He didn't say who it was."

Nate set his pen down, his frustration showing. "Elijah, we need to know who that is."

"I was pushing my luck as it was," Elijah pleaded.

"It's okay, son," said Sarah. "You did fine."

"You did fine," said Nate apologetically.

"Hey!" Elisha brightened with recollection. "Norman said Jim Boltz and his three friends used to pick on Ian Snyder. *Three* friends."

Nate leaned back in his chair, digesting that. "So we have a gang of four, but only three got sick."

Elijah offered, "If all four picked on Ian, then all four would have been on his list."

"And most likely on the list of the soda-straw planter." Nate almost jumped out of his chair. "Let's talk to Tom Gessner. He might know who number four is."

∾

Blake Hornsby was a handsome senior, a letterman, and a surprisingly polite young man. Apparently, he'd already done quite a bit of soul-searching before he got called into Tom Gessner's office. He was close to tears.

"I'm sorry," he said, his voice choked with emotion. "I didn't mean to hurt anybody. It's just that, you know, everybody does it. It's like it's part of going to school, you know? You get razzed when you're a freshman, and then you turn around and razz the freshmen when you're a senior, stuff like that."

"Did you ever pick on Ian Snyder?" Nate asked him, sitting close, speaking gently. He was still wearing his janitor's coveralls, but he'd revealed to Blake why he and his family were there.

Blake nodded emphatically and confessed, "Oh, yeah. We all did. Every chance we got. We knocked his books out of his hands, we pulled his hair—we were going to cut it off once, but then we thought we'd get in trouble for having a pair of scissors.

That can be considered a weapon, you know? We stole his stuff and tossed it around. Broke his watch once."

Gessner asked, "Blake, did it ever occur to you that you might be hurting a fellow human being?"

He shrugged. "You don't think about it. You're with the other guys, and they go after somebody, and you know, you do the same thing, you have some fun." Then he added, angry with himself, "But it was stupid. Bunch of guys trying to look tough, I guess, but it was stupid. I can't believe I did it." He turned to Sarah. "What's going to happen to the guys? I tried to visit them in the hospital, but the doctors wouldn't let me in. They've got the room quarantined."

Sarah answered, "Tod is comatose. If we don't find out what this is within the next day or so, he'll probably be joining Amy and Crystal."

Blake couldn't hold back his tears.

Nate asked, "Blake, we need to know who else you and the others have picked on. We have to know the extent of this and who else was involved."

Blake wiped his eyes. "Nelson Parker." He chuckled, even through his tears. "He's got acne, you know. He's got it bad!" Tom Gessner wrote the name down. "But we didn't go real hard on the guy, it was just teasing. He never looked like we were killing him or anything."

"Who else?" Gessner asked.

"There was Crystal."

"Already got her down."

"And the rest of the witchy bunch."

"The witchy bunch?"

"You know, Ian's weird friends." Blake named three of them, and then remembered, "Oh, and Norman Bloom, too. We call him the rat man."

Gessner explained to the Springfields, "Norman's a T.A. in Mr. Harrigan's biology class. He takes care of the lab animals."

Sarah nodded. "Elisha knows him."

"But we haven't bothered him in a while," said Blake. "I mean, it got to the point where he was paying us to leave him alone, and that got to be too much."

Nate locked eyes with Blake. "He *paid* you to leave him alone?"

Blake was ashamed to admit it. "Yeah. He'd give us ten dollars, and we'd ease up for a week."

It was difficult for Gessner and the Springfields to conceal their disgust. Gessner finally said, "Blake, do you know what extortion is?"

"Uh, I guess so."

"It's what you and your friends did to Norman, that's what it is."

"Yeah."

"Do you plan to give that money back?"

Blake thought a moment, then quickly answered, "Yeah. Every penny."

"I'm sure you will." It wasn't an observation. It was an order.

"Who else?" Nate asked.

"Brenda Smith," Blake answered. "She's ugly."

Sarah could feel the indignant mother rising in her. "And you felt it was your duty to make that judgment. By now I imagine she's thoroughly convinced of it."

Blake looked scolded. "I guess I'd better tell her I'm sorry."

Nate nodded, somewhat sternly. "I think that would be a wise idea."

Tom Gessner asked, "Who else?"

Blake supplied just two more names and then said, "And, I guess all the freshmen."

Gessner sighed, clicking his pen closed. "Don't worry about remembering their names. I can get a list."

"Is that it?" Blake asked.

"One more thing," said Nate. "We have to search your locker."

He half shrugged. "I gotta warn you, it's a mess. I haven't cleaned it out all year. But can I ask you something?"

"Sure."

"I think I've got one of those little hanging-man symbols on the locker door. Is that, you know, for *real?*"

ᕀᕿᕟ

Blake had had that symbol on his locker since before Jim Boltz became ill, but he hadn't paid much attention to it. After all, unless you looked at it carefully, it looked like just another scratch, and every locker in the school had plenty of those. Even the Springfields had missed it the first time.

But it was there, all right, just like the others.

Mr. Maxwell's nose picked up a particular scent before they'd even gotten the locker door open, and he began whining, tugging at his leash to get closer. He was so excited that they had to secure his leash to a doorknob across the hall.

"Steady, boy, steady," said Nate, scratching his ears. "You'll get your chance."

Nate and Sarah moved quickly and carefully, emptying the contents bit by bit, coat by tennis racket by book by running shoe, into plastic bags on the floor.

Blake stood by and watched, fascinated and a little anxious. "What are you looking for, anyway?"

"Whatever we find," said Nate.

Sarah lifted a wadded-up windbreaker from the floor of the locker, then a gym towel, then some hot-rod magazines, and then she spotted it.

A soda straw.

"Bingo," she said, picking it up with tweezers. She smelled it herself, then wrinkled her nose. "Max?"

Nate untied Max's leash from the doorknob and brought him over. Max took one sniff of the straw and went crazy, dancing, tugging at the leash, barking, looking at Nate and Sarah as if to say, *That's it! That's it! Can't you smell that?*

While Nate secured Max to the doorknob again and gave him a treat—half to reward him and half to quiet him down—Sarah asked Blake, "How long has all this stuff been in the bottom of your locker?"

"Uh, couple weeks, I guess."

She looked at Nate. "This thing's been buried down there at least that long."

Nate clicked on his flashlight and illuminated the straw as she examined it. "But what's different about this one? Max didn't alert at the others."

Sarah glanced up at Blake Hornsby, standing there healthy and normal. "And it didn't seem to work either." She peered at the straw through a magnifying glass as Nate kept his light on it. "Sugar crystals again. We'll probably find Tricanol, just as before." Her brow furrowed. "Waaaiiiit a minute."

She turned the straw and looked in the other end. "Ohhh wow . . ."

"What is it?" Blake asked.

She let Nate look down the end of the straw. He whistled in awe.

"Bag," she said. "BAG!"

Nate held a plastic bag open and she dropped in the straw. Then she yanked off her surgical gloves and grabbed her cell phone. She strained to remember. "Oh, what's his number, what's his number?"

Nate already had his pocket organizer in hand. "Who're you calling?"

"Algernon Wheeling."

He raised his eyebrows just a moment, then looked up the number.

She peered at the straw through a magnifying glass as Nate kept his light on it.

9

ALGERNON
WHEELING

THAT AFTERNOON, NATE and Sarah cleared a large area of the Holy Roller and set out the clothing, books, magazines, shoes, jackets, duffel bags, and anything else that once belonged to the victims. They mixed in some of their own clothes and some they'd bought at the local Goodwill, along with any books, handbags, backpacks, and personal items they could scrounge from the local grade school. Then they brought in Mr. Maxwell to play his favorite game: tracking down a scent in exchange for a biscuit.

"Okay, boy, here you go." Sarah opened the plastic bag and let him sniff the last straw, the *ultimate* straw taken from Blake Hornsby's locker. Then she turned him loose and he bolted for all those wonderful, smelly things arranged in neat rows on the motor home floor.

It wasn't a very challenging game. Max found the scent on the first article he encountered, Crystal Sparks' leather handbag. He found it on Amy Warren's jacket, on Jim Boltz's shirt, on Leonard Baynes' wallet. He found it on shoelaces, handkerchiefs, notebooks, a hairbrush, a few magazines. Nate and Sarah almost thought he was bluffing them, but noted that he did not find the scent on any of the "neutral" items they'd planted among the others. Nate removed any item Max tagged, and Sarah made a note of it. Before long, Max was circling the room, his nose leading the way, but finding nothing. He began to whine.

Nate stepped up with two biscuits. Max had more than earned them. "Good boy, Max. Good boy."

Max got his reward and took it outside to enjoy.

Nate removed his disposable gloves and looked at Sarah.

She merely shook her head, looking at the separated items on the table and then her notes. "Whatever it is, it gets around."

"From hand to object, from object to hand," Nate observed. "The hairbrush, the books, the tote bags, the wallet. Everything with the scent on it was handled at one time by someone."

"So the scent spreads like germs. Person to person, surface to surface. And it lasts, too. Some of this stuff hasn't been touched in over two weeks."

"And now the million-dollar question is, where'd the scent come from? We've only found it in that one soda straw. The others have a different scent altogether."

"And Tod Kramer's clothing has the scent, but we never found a soda straw among his belongings or in his locker."

"Algernon might be able to tell us. When's he getting here?"

"He's catching a red-eye flight tonight and should be here early tomorrow morning." She heard Nate huff a sigh. "I know. We can't wait."

Nate drew another deep breath. Now he was feeling like

Max, tugging at a leash and unable to leap forward. "Well, okay, we'll get all the information we can so Algernon will have something to work with." He went to the dinette table and unrolled the old blueprints of the school. "In the meantime, I'm intrigued by the location of Amy's and Crystal's lockers. Did you notice this?"

Sarah came over to look.

"Here's the location of Blake Hornsby's locker on the main floor, right near the gym, just around the corner from the Forbidden Hallway. Now look at this . . ." He turned that page aside, revealing the plans for the upper floor of the school. "Here's Amy Warren's locker, and here's Crystal's. They're within ten feet of each other, but directly above Blake Hornsby's locker, and—"

The door to the motor home opened, and Elijah and Elisha came in, packs on their backs, faces rosy from the walk home from school. They immediately noticed all the stuff spread out on the floor, and Elijah asked, "So, how'd it go?"

"Pretty much as we expected," Sarah answered.

Elijah eyed the ultimate soda straw, now sealed again in a plastic bag on Sarah's lab table. "Have you heard from Professor Wheeling?"

"He'll be here tomorrow morning," said Nate.

"Dad!" Elisha gasped excitedly. "I may have thought of something!" She hurried to the dinette table, where the school blueprints were already spread out. "Did you notice where Amy's and Crystal's lockers are? They're right above Blake Hornsby's!"

Nate and Sarah were amused but pleased. "Go on," said Nate.

Elisha pointed to the blueprints. "Look here. There's an old shaft running up the wall behind the lockers. Mr. Loman says it used to be a cold-air return for the furnace when the old building was still there. Check it out." She turned back to the previous page. "See? It's right behind Blake Hornsby's locker on the first floor, and Amy's and Crystal's lockers on the second floor. It would be a perfect passageway for something to move upward from the first floor to the second."

Nate and Sarah exchanged a look. "Go on," said Sarah.

"I looked at the wall above Amy's and Crystal's lockers, and there's a vent up there. It's kind of small and tight, but a smaller person could fit through it."

Nate cocked a fatherly eyebrow. "And just why would a smaller person want to do that?"

Elisha got impatient. "To check out a theory! I want to see if there's a physical connection between Blake's locker and the girls' lockers upstairs."

"And if there is?" Sarah asked.

Elisha was starting to sound like a salesgirl making a pitch. "Then it might bolster my theory that whatever didn't get to Blake Hornsby went upstairs and got to the girls instead, and that's why they got sick and he didn't."

A short, silent moment passed as Nate and Sarah thought it over. Nate took a studious second look at the blueprints, his arms folded across his chest.

Finally, he said, "Elisha, better step cautiously. We're still not sure what we're dealing with."

"I understand." But she was still excited.

Nate thought a moment longer. "Okay. Work with Mr. Loman on this. He'll know the best way to get in there without running into trouble. You'll have to wear protective clothing, and I mean head to toe, gloves, hood, the works."

Elisha dropped her backpack. "I can wear that toxic substance suit, that EPA thing. It's in the rear cargo hold!" She headed for the door.

"But first—!"

She turned, her hand on the knob.

"Plan this for tomorrow morning before classes—and *after* we've had a chance to discuss this with Professor Wheeling."

That didn't deter her one bit. "Got it!" She was out the door.

Sarah was concerned. "Nate, are you sure?"

He shrugged, a twinkle in his eye. "It's her theory, and she's right: She's the only one small enough. But we'll wait and see what Algernon has to say before we carry this any further. In the meantime, Elijah . . ."

"Sir?"

"Now that Max knows—and we know—what to sniff for, I can just about predict that Professor Wheeling is going to want Max to sniff out the whole school."

Elijah gave a little whistle. "That's going to be a big job. Where do we even start?"

Nate lightly drummed his fingers on his chin. "Old Abel Frye went after the athletes first, so I'd like to start in the boys' locker room at the gym."

Elijah chuckled. "There are *plenty* of smells in there!"

Nate's face crinkled up a bit—he was still thinking. "Besides, don't the guys get assigned lockers in the gym classes?"

"Oh, yes."

"Then Tod Kramer's hall locker wasn't the only locker he used."

That turned Sarah's head. "Another drop point for a soda straw! We should have thought of that!"

"I just did," said Nate. "A little *late*, maybe, but . . . Elijah, tomorrow morning we'll bring Max to school and check it out. Which means"—he smiled knowingly at his son—"I'll get a chance to meet that good friend of yours, Mr. Marquardt."

Elijah made a face. "Oh, you're gonna love him!"

₧₧

The next morning came early, *too* early, and all four Springfields were beginning to feel the wear and exhaustion of the last several days as they dragged themselves out of bed. Nevertheless, as soon as the kids were awake enough to know it, the adrenaline began to flow and they couldn't wait to get out the door. Sarah had to remind them to eat their breakfast.

"I'm going to run out of time," said Elisha, scarfing down her oatmeal and raisins.

"Take it easy, girl," Sarah cautioned.

"First things first, second things second," Nate reminded

them. "Elisha, you can't explore that shaft until we've had a chance to talk to Professor Wheeling. And Elijah, you can't bring Max into the school gym until I've had a chance to prepare Mr. Marquardt."

They settled down a little, or at least tried to. Elijah savored his Wheat Chex, Elisha finished her oatmeal at a better-mannered pace.

Time passed. Then it passed some more. They all noticed.

"When's Professor Wheeling supposed to get here?" Elisha asked.

Sarah looked unhappily at the clock. "A half-hour ago."

"Maybe his plane was late," Nate suggested. "Did he have clear directions?"

Sarah rose from the table and went to the telephone. "I'll call the airline and see what's up."

Elisha was also watching the clock. "Mr. Loman is going to be waiting for me."

Nate finished the last few drops from his coffee cup and set it down. "And Mr. Marquardt is going to be waiting for *me*. Elisha, go ahead and gather up your gear, and grab one of the radios." Elisha leaped up from the table and Nate quickly added, "Stay in communication and don't proceed until we give you clearance, got it?"

"Yes, sir. Got it."

"Hello? Southwest?" Sarah was on the phone with the airline.

Elisha went out the door. Nate grabbed his coat, his Stetson hat, and his tool bag. "Elijah, go ahead and bring Max to the school in . . ." He looked at his watch. "An hour."

Elijah looked at his own watch. "School will be starting by then."

Nate shrugged. "Looks like you'll have to be absent from classes today." He went out the door.

Elijah had a few spoonfuls of Wheat Chex remaining and no immediate need to abandon them, so he just kept eating.

☙❧

Nate pushed his way through the big swinging door that led into the boys' locker room, and after one breath there could be no mistaking where he was. The cool air, permanently dank from the dripping showers, carried an unforgettable mixture of scents: the concrete floor, the wooden benches, the metal lockers, the hundreds of once-sweaty tee shirts, and the rubbery-smelling gym shoes stored in the basket room.

The place echoed. All the walls were concrete block painted a dull green. A fan was running somewhere.

He rounded a corner and walked along the lockers until he came to the gym office, situated between the locker room and the gym. He could see a man inside, sitting at his desk and reading over some stat sheets. The man wore gray trousers and a light blue jacket, and a whistle hung by a chain around his neck. He was youthful, muscular, and striking a very confident pose. This had to be Mr. Marquardt.

The door was open. Nate removed his hat and knocked on the doorjamb. "Hello. Mr. Marquardt?"

Marquardt looked up from his desk and looked Nate over with a sneering, judgmental eye. "What are you supposed to be, some kind of cowboy?"

Nate smiled. "I'm Nate Springfield. And yes, I grew up on a cattle ranch in Montana."

Marquardt finally smiled and ordered with a jerk of his head, "Have a seat."

"Thank you." Nate sat in an available chair. "I understand Ms. Wyrthen told you I'd be coming?"

"She told me. Said you were some kind of investigator. I thought you were a janitor."

"Well, I've swept a few floors and emptied a few trash cans in the course of things. But we're close to wrapping up this investigation, and we need your help."

Marquardt rotated his chair to face Nate directly, then leaned back with an almost haughty air of confidence. "So what can I do for you?"

ൟ

Elisha arrived in the second-floor hallway and found Mr. Loman waiting with a ladder already up against the wall, the grille over the old cold-air return vent removed.

"Well, good morning, Miss Springfield! And don't you look ready for—well, for something, I don't know what!"

Elisha was wearing a bright orange coverall suit, complete with boots, gloves, and a hood she carried under her arm. On her waist was a palm-sized radio with a headset, and in a bag she carried small tools, a set of building plans, and a head-mounted flashlight, the same one she had used in the Forbidden Hallway several nights ago. "Good morning, Mr. Loman."

"You look like you're ready to go to the moon."

"Well . . .." She began searching through her bag. "I might be ready to clean up a toxic waste area, I suppose. Oh, *no!*"

"Got a problem?"

"I forgot to bring fresh batteries for my headlamp! I can't believe it!"

"Well, we must have some fresh batteries around here somewhere. How about the stock room for bio-chem? I opened it up for Norman just a few minutes ago. You know Norman?"

Elisha brightened. "Norman? Sure."

❧

Professor Algernon Wheeling was late, a bit flustered, but still basically jolly when he pulled up alongside the Holy Roller in his rental car and tooted his horn.

Sarah hopped down from the motor home and broke into a wide grin. "Well! You made it!"

"Professor Sarah, we meet again!" Algernon climbed out of the car, his briefcase already in his hand. He was a short little man in his fifties, gray and balding, with thick glasses. His eyes seemed to look two different directions at once, but his friendly, toothy grin brought your attention back to center immediately. "We can blame a variety of people for my lateness. I can blame myself for trying to bring so much equipment on the plane. I can blame the airline for hassling me about it. I can blame air-traffic control for making us hold on the runway for so long. But—" He shrugged happily. "God bless me, I am here at last!"

They shook hands, and then decided a hug would be even better.

"So how are things in entomology?" she asked.

Algernon climbed out of the car, his briefcase already in his hand. He was a short little man in his fifties, gray and balding, with thick glasses. His eyes seemed to look two different directions at once, but his friendly, toothy grin brought your attention back to center immediately.

"Oh, just buzzing. Get it? Buzzing?" Then he became serious—sort of. "But things are buzzing here, too, I understand."

She nodded grimly. "Time's at a premium. We've lost two kids, and now the hospital is bringing in specialists and the police are pulling everyone they can to put them on this case. They're all waiting for what you might find out."

He rolled his eyes, impatient with himself. "So why am I standing here? Come on, Wheeling, get with the program." He spun around and opened the rear car door. "From what you told me on the phone, I'd say yes, you've found a pheromone, a scent that an insect gives off—you know, squirts, smears, spits—in order to send a message to other insects." He pulled out some heavy cloth cases, set them on the ground, and then laughed at himself. "Yeah, real good, Wheeling! Tell the lady something she doesn't know!"

"But have you ever encountered anything like this?" Sarah asked. "It seems to stick to everything and lasts for weeks."

Algernon filled his hands and arms with cases of various sizes and weights as Sarah grabbed whatever was left. "Oh, it's not too unusual. Ants mark their trails with scent markers that can last for weeks. Dogs can smell the urine of another dog for at least that long." He nodded toward the motor home. "Uh, so . . ."

"Right this way," she said. As they approached the door of the motor home, they met Elijah coming out. "Algernon, you remember my son, Elijah."

He stood still a moment and gawked at Elijah, his eyes seemingly looking at either side of him. "I could say, 'My, how you've grown,' but you already know that, don't you?"

"Hello, Professor Wheeling."

Sarah explained as Elijah passed by them and they went into the motor home, "We're in a real rush this morning. Elijah has to take Mr. Maxwell to the school to do some nasal reconnaissance."

"Nasal reconnaissance!" Algernon got a kick out of that.

Elijah untied Mr. Maxwell and they started walking together toward the school. Yes, that was Professor Wheeling all right.

∽

Using a strong flashlight, and with surgical gloves on his hands, Nate examined the seams around the floor of locker number 106 while Mr. Marquardt stood over him, half curious and half skeptical.

"Like I said," said Marquardt, "I get somebody to clean out these lockers every week, so I doubt you're going to find anything."

"Who cleans them out?" Nate asked, now using a magnifying glass.

"Oh, whoever needs a little punishment."

"But you're sure this was Tod Kramer's locker?"

"Oh yeah, 106, fourth period, Tod Kramer."

Uh-oh. Nate moved his magnifying glass nearer, farther,

back and forth, peering intensely. He quickly prepared a small length of double-back tape on the end of a toothpick and used it to extract a very tiny, crystalline object from the crack formed where the floor of the locker met the rear wall. When he brought it out into the light and had a better look at it, he nodded jubilantly. It was a tiny clump of sugar crystals, no doubt tainted with Tricanol. The soda straw had been cleaned out, but this little tidbit managed to remain. "Abel Frye" had been here. He dropped the sample into a tiny, sterile vial, tightened on the cap, and stowed it in his tool bag.

"So, Tod Kramer was in your fourth-period class."

"That's right."

"Did he ever pick on anybody?"

Marquardt scowled. "What kind of a question is that?"

Nate found himself trying to be patient. He rephrased the question. "To your knowledge, did Tod Kramer ever harass, abuse, bully, tease, shove, humiliate, you know, pick on anybody?"

Marquardt smirked a little. "I'm sure he did. A lot of them do."

"Would you have any idea *whom* he picked on?"

"I don't pay attention to that kind of stuff."

Nate didn't like hearing an answer like that from a teacher. "You don't?"

He seemed indignant at the question. "Listen. I'm here to teach, to make sure these boys come out of this school physically fit. I'm not here to baby-sit or counsel or hold little weaklings by the hand. Have you ever tried to teach a high school gym class?"

"No, sir."

"It's a cage full of animals. They need to be controlled; they need to be whipped into shape. If you get soft, if you start listening to excuses and feeling sorry for whiners, the class falls apart."

"So you do what's necessary to maintain control."

Marquardt gave a deep, sarcastic nod. "Now you're getting the picture!"

"But if I hear you correctly, you see no need to control abuse and harassment among your students?" Marquardt looked away, giving his head a little shake as if he were talking with a naïve child. Nate decided to clarify his question. "Mr. Marquardt, two students are dead and four are dying, and in most cases it could be because they've made enemies. We're trying to find out who those enemies are."

"Then you must be after that Snyder kid, am I right?"

"I'll be honest with you, Mr. Marquardt. We're taking a look at him."

Marquardt smiled a mean smile. "He's your man. That kid's nothing but trouble."

"Do you think Ian Snyder would have reason to want to harm Tod Kramer?"

Now Marquardt laughed. "You better believe it!"

જ્જ

Algernon sat at Sarah's worktable, gazing through head-mounted magnifying glasses as he carefully dissected the soda straw with a scalpel. "Uh-huh, yes, yes, right on the money. Now we're cooking with gas . . ."

He cut a portion of the straw away, then held it to his nose. "Female. Definitely female." He looked over his magnifiers at Sarah, who sat beside him. "So we had a female inside this straw. She was squirting her pheromone all over the inside of it, trying to attract a male. That's what Max was smelling. That's what you have on all these items belonging to the victims. Some pheromones are so sticky they spread like head lice."

Sarah considered the long list of scented objects. "Looks like we could also have a lot of females in a lot of places."

"And that would be bad news, Sarah. Bad news. So we press on . . ."

From his tool kit, he grabbed a jeweler's tool—a long, skinny little gadget with four grabbing fingers at one end, operated by pressing a plunger at the other end. He carefully inserted it into the straw, muttering to himself. "Like poor Rapunzel, trapped in a tower . . . waiting for Prince Charming . . ." He began to withdraw the grabbing tool, slowly, slowly. "And herrrrrre . . . he . . . is."

Sarah put on her own pair of magnifying glasses and looked as Algernon held a little tangle of brown fuzzy shards under the light.

"Mm-hm," he said, turning the little grabber and gazing through his magnifiers. "Two walking legs, one pedipalp, and

. . . an anterior portion of the cephalothorax. All that's left."

Sarah didn't understand. "All that's left?"

He explained. "Leftovers. Somebody put a female in this straw and then sealed her in with two plugs made of sugar. She put out her pheromone, her scent, to attract a male, and this guy right here came calling. He burrowed his way through a sugar plug, mated with her—it's not very exciting, kind of like throwing a McDonald's hamburger into a glove box—and then . . ." He looked over his magnifiers at her. "She ate him. These are the pieces left over."

"She *ate* him?"

He set the grabber tool in a stand and dollied his wheeled chair over to his notebook computer. "Not uncommon among spiders. The black widow likes to have her lovers for lunch. But this poor guy . . ." He began tapping on the computer keys. "He wasn't a black widow. He looks more like a brown recluse. They're poisonous and pretty rare in this part of the country." An image came up on the screen—a gruesome, detailed electron photograph of a spider with black, multiple eyes, sharp claws, and bristly hairs. Algernon examined the computer image, then wheeled over for another look at the spider parts under the light. "Yeah. Bingo. Brown recluse."

Then he straightened up in his chair as if startled by a thought. "God help us." Then he sat there, staring as if in a trance.

Sarah asked, "Algernon? What is it?"

He snapped out of it, but now he was agitated. "I don't want to speak too soon. But here . . ." He hurried over and started unlatching another of his tool cases. "Help me get this sniffer set up. Is the school in session today?"

"Yes."

That jerked his head around, his eyes wide with horror. "It is?"

10

A LETHAL
COMBINATION

ELISHA, STILL COVERED up to the neck in a bright orange safety suit, quickly returned from the bio-chem department, fresh batteries in hand. Norman Bloom, overcome with curiosity, was walking beside her and would not be dissuaded.

"I mean, it's a little strange seeing a girl from biology class wearing a protective suit to school," he was saying.

"Norman," Elisha admitted, "I'm actually here to do some investigating."

"Investigating? Investigating what?"

"We're checking the cold-air return," Mr. Loman told him. He'd already used that answer on some early arriving kids who'd passed by and asked what the opened vent and ladder were all about. He looked at his watch and told Elisha, "Come on, climb in there before anybody else sees you in that getup. We're gonna have a ton of traffic in just a few minutes."

Elisha hesitated. "I can't. I have to wait for clearance."

"Clearance?"

Elisha nervously, self-consciously tinkered with the radio on her belt. "I have to hear from home first."

"To check a furnace duct?" Norman asked, chuckling at the whole bizarre situation. "What's going on here?"

Elisha put on the headset and spoke into it. "Hello, Mom? This is Elisha. We're ready to go when you are." No answer came back. "Hello? Mom? Are you there?"

Mr. Loman looked at his watch, then suddenly blurted, "Norman, we're looking for some kind of bug."

Norman made a face. "A bug?"

Elisha could feel her face flush with anger. "Mr. Loman! If you don't mind—"

Mr. Loman asked Norman, "Norman, you know spiders and bugs, right?"

"Sure."

Mr. Loman unclipped his flashlight from his belt and handed it to him. "Okay, up the ladder. We need you to crawl down that shaft and tell us if you see anything unusual."

Elisha was horrified. "Mr. Loman! You can't do that!"

Mr. Loman only looked at his watch again. "Well, I'm sorry, Elisha, but the time to do this is right now, and you don't have clearance, whatever that means. This school's going to be crammed with kids in just a few minutes and this ladder could be a safety hazard. If Ms. Wyrthen finds out I had this ladder out in the hall during school hours she'll can me!"

"You want me to look for *spiders?*" Norman asked, still bewildered.

"Spiders, bugs, whatever. You do know what a bug looks like, don't you?"

Norman got indignant. "I most certainly do. I've collected several specimens and—"

"Up the ladder."

"Norman!" Elisha countered. "Don't go! It could be dangerous!"

He brushed that off. "Elisha! I know insects. I know what to look for. Don't worry." He started up the ladder. "What if I get dirty?"

"You get to go home and change," said Mr. Loman.

Norman headed up the ladder as Elisha stood there helplessly, watching someone else bump her from *her* adventure. She got on her radio again. "Mom! I'd be ever so pleased if you would *answer!*"

◯◯◯

Nate and Mr. Marquardt were back in the gym office, Marquardt at his desk, Nate in an available chair. Marquardt seemed to draw strength from being in his office, kind of like a king in his own little throne room.

"Stupid kid," he was saying. "Wears a dangly earring in P.E. class. One of these days somebody's gonna rip that thing out."

"Somebody like Tod Kramer?"

Marquardt stayed cool as he slowly nodded. "If Snyder asks for it one too many times, yeah."

"So Ian and Tod *were* in the same fourth-period gym class, is that right?"

"That's right."

"And Tod abused Ian Snyder on occasion?"

Marquardt actually seemed amused. "On *occasion?*"

Nate consulted the class schedule they'd gotten from the school office. "Well now. Brock Hanley's in your fourth-period class, too. He's your teaching assistant."

Marquardt turned defensive. "So what's *he* done?"

"Oh . . . found an interesting way to get lunch money." Nate found a name that almost startled him. "*Norman Bloom* is in fourth period!"

That name brought a derisive sniff from Mr. Marquardt. "Bloom," he muttered disgustedly.

"You seem to have a low opinion of Mr. Bloom."

"He's a wimp."

That stopped Nate in his tracks. "Norman Bloom is a *wimp?*"

"Sure. All his growth hormones went to his brain. The kid can't throw a football." He laughed. "He can't even *hold* a football."

"Have you told him that?"

"I let the boys know when they can do better, you bet."

"Did Tod Kramer or Brock Hanley ever pick on Bloom?"

Marquardt tilted his head as if ready to scold a child. "Oh, are we sticking up for Bloom now?"

Nate reminded himself to keep cool, go slowly, speak gently. "I've been hired to track down what's happened to some kids in this school, some of whom were your star athletes, which means I have to find a culprit and a motive, which means I have to find out if any of the victims had enemies, which means I have to ask questions about people like Tod Kramer and Brock Hanley and whomever they may have picked on."

"And my answer's going to be the same for all of them!"

Marquardt's temper was starting to show. "Every kid in my classes gets an even break. Every kid gets the same pressure. We push them to produce, we don't accept excuses, we require maximum effort. If the strong prey upon the weak at times, so be it, that's part of their education. That's life talking. That's the way the world is. It's what makes us tough. Just read your science book, Mr. Springfield. This is a world of winners and losers. The weak toughen up, or they fall behind; the strong prevail, and we're all better off. Maybe people like you don't like it, but that's the way it works."

Nate began to pity this man. "That's quite a philosophy, Mr. Marquardt."

"It's how I've survived, Mr. Springfield. It's how I fought my way through school and got where I am today. It's how all of us have to survive. We live in a lousy world in case you haven't noticed, and I'm not about to shelter anyone. The tough survive. It's as simple as that." Then he added with more than a hint of pride, "The tough win games, too. You may have heard, we're heading for the championship on Turkey Day."

"Without your star quarterback?"

"The tough survive, Mr. Springfield. We'll be ready, make no mistake."

"The tough survive," Nate repeated thoughtfully. "So if one kid abuses and harasses another, that's fine with you?"

"I let the kids work it out. That's the way you and I have to do it. They may as well get used to it."

Nate drew a long, careful breath and then spoke in a low, very controlled tone of voice, his eyes locked on Marquardt's. "Mr.

Marquardt, I've never taught a gym class, but I've spent years investigating crime scenes—you know, the aftermath of the strong and ruthless preying upon the weak and innocent. I've had to smell death, sample blood, reconstruct in pencil or clay what people used to look like before they were beaten to death so the police can even guess who they were. Now maybe you consider that 'life,' the way things are, something everybody has to get used to, but let me tell you something: Cruelty is no sign of manliness, and having dealt with the results of cruelty for years, I can assure you, you never get used to it. Now . . ." Nate repeated the question Marquardt hadn't answered. "I still need to know, did Tod Kramer ever pick on Norman Bloom?"

As if to make a point, Marquardt laughed. "*Of course* he did! What do you expect?"

⊘⊘

Mr. Loman stood at the top of the ladder and hollered into the open vent. "How's it going, Norman?"

From where she stood below, Elisha could hear a faint, echoing voice replying, but she couldn't understand what Norman said.

"Okay, fine," said Mr. Loman. He called down to Elisha, "He's reached the bottom. Now what do you want him to find out?"

Elisha was looking at the building plans, trying desperately to make the best of it, but mortified and angry. "Tell him . . ." She had to take a breath and calm herself. "Tell him if there seems to be a visible connection between . . . I mean, ask him—" She got on the radio. "Mom? Hello?"

Mr. Loman called down the shaft, "Do you see any *spiders,* Norman?" His tone seemed to mock Elisha, as if she were a timid girl afraid of spiders.

Elisha heard Norman's off-handed reply. "Sure."

"Well, don't let 'em getcha."

There was a metallic groan, then a clatter.

"What's up, Norman?"

A hollow clunk.

"Norman? What're you doing?"

No answer.

"Norman?"

Elisha gripped the ladder and listened.

Mr. Loman called more loudly, "Norman?"

No answer.

ℰ𝒳ℐ

Algernon Wheeling plugged in his "sniffer" and turned it on. It was a black box the size and shape of a VCR, with digital readouts on the front, rows of tiny silver knobs, and a small wand that resembled a microphone on a cord. The wand was the actual "sniffer," a receptor for airborne molecules that noses interpret as smells.

"A dog like Mr. Maxwell is still the most practical way to go," Algernon conceded, "but a dog can't tell you exactly what molecules are in a smell, or exactly who left it there. This machine can. And so . . ."

He held the wand over the soda straw that had contained the

female spider, and the machine began to blink out rows of numbers on its readout. Just a few feet away, a computer printer began to reel off data. The moment the printing was completed, Algernon grabbed up the paper and studied it. "Don't be, don't be, come on now . . ."

"What are you looking for?" Sarah asked. She could recognize many of the chemical formulas, but only Algernon knew what they meant.

"What I desperately hope not to find," he answered. He set the sheet of paper on the worktable and grabbed up a reference manual filled with more formulas, more numbers. He flipped through the pages hurriedly, frantically. "00-2-9975, Category 5 . . ." He flipped some more pages, forward, backward, searching. "No, no, too wide a band . . ." Flip flip.

His finger landed on a page and stopped there. His eyes went from the printout to the manual and back again, comparing, comparing.

He sat down, the manual open in his hand, his finger still on the page. "Mmmmm-hm. African spotted wolf. Sarah, could you please call the hospital? I need to talk to the physician in charge of the victims."

Sarah grabbed the telephone and dialed a direct number Dr. Stuart had given her. "Hello? Dr. Stuart? Sarah Springfield. I'm going to hand you over to Algernon Wheeling, professor of entomology at the University of Washington."

She handed the receiver to Algernon.

"Hello?" he said. "Dr. Stuart? Hello, sir. Very well, thank you. Do you mow your own lawn, sir? Yes, sir, I am serious. Okay. Do you put the grass clippings in a pile somewhere? All right. So you know what hot, composting grass smells like? Okay, great. I'm ecstatic. Can you do something for me? Check your patients' breath, smell their skin, particularly under the arms. We're looking for that smell—oh, and could you check the base of their gums? There should be a concentration of greenish plaque under there with the same odor. Okay, we're standing by." He addressed Sarah. "He's checking."

"And if he finds it?" Sarah asked.

Algernon gave a shudder. "It'll be the Kenyan disaster all over again."

◌

Mr. Loman looked worried. "Norman!" He eyed the vent opening. There was no way *he* would fit through.

Elisha made a decision. She dropped the building plans on the floor, then put on her protective hood and headlamp. "Excuse me, Mr. Loman."

He took his cue and hurried down off the ladder.

Elisha spoke into her radio. "Mom, we have an emergency. I have to go in. Call me when you can." She clambered up to the opening, clicked on her head-mounted lamp, and crawled through.

◌

Elijah and Mr. Maxwell arrived at the school just as the buses were pulling up. This was going to complicate things a little. Everyone was going to wonder what he was doing with a dog in school.

Just then, Trevor and Carl, Elijah's two buddies from calculus, got off a bus.

"Hey! Nice dog!"

"Is that yours?"

Elijah was trying to figure out how he would explain even as he answered, "Yeah, sure is."

They looked at him strangely, then exchanged a glance with each other. Carl said, "Elijah, is there something going on here? I mean, first you hang out with Ian Snyder, and now you bring a dog to school."

Elijah looked them both in the eye and admitted, "Yeah. There's something going on. Could you kind of . . . play along for a while? I'll tell you all about it when it's over."

They looked at each other, made faces that meant they were impressed, then hurried into the building.

"Okay, Max," Elijah said, leading Max up the stairs toward the main door, "it's now or never."

Elisha made a decision. She dropped the building plans on the floor, then put on her protective hood and headlamp.

"Excuse me, Mr. Loman."

❧

Algernon was a bundle of nervous energy as he waited for Dr. Stuart to return to the phone. Pressing the receiver to his ear with his shoulder, he swiveled in his chair and began tapping the keys on his computer. "The, uh, the brown recluse has a distant cousin in East Africa, the African spotted wolf—that's not a dog, it's the name of a poisonous spider. The poison works slowly, causing paranoia, then hallucinations, then dementia—you know, the victim goes crazy, babbling nonsense, fleeing from everything, being generally out of his mind, just like the victims in this case—are you with me, Sarah?"

"I'm with you."

"Some of the primitive tribes in Africa found a way to use the poison against their enemies. The poison could eventually kill them, but not before they went crazy and killed each other. It was a perfect weapon."

He tapped one final key, and an image formed on the computer screen. "The African spotted wolf. Not big as spiders go, less than half a centimeter. The bite hardly leaves a mark—but you've seen what it can do."

Sarah stared at the greatly magnified image with loathing. It was a thin, spindly thing, brownish-red with black spots, slick in appearance.

Algernon responded to a voice on the telephone. "Yes, hello." He listened, then sighed, his shoulders dropping. "Yes, sir. Thank you. That's good news and bad news. We'll get right back to you.

Yes, as soon as we have something. Thank you, doctor." He handed the receiver to Sarah, who hung it up. He pointed to his computer screen. "We've found the culprit."

꘎

The old airshaft was dusty and filled with decades of spider webs. Sure. Just as Norman had replied, there were spiders in here. There had always been spiders in here. Suddenly the whole question of finding spiders in this place seemed a bit silly, like going to an ocean beach to find out if there was any sand.

The shaft was like a square box, framed from aging two-by-fours and plywood, and only a few feet across. It was difficult for Elisha to move her body, to bend, reach, or turn. Hanging by one hand from the lip of the vent opening, she raised the face shield of her hood for a better view downward, tilting her head to direct the beam of her headlamp. It was like looking down a square, bottomless well. The dirty, cobwebbed walls dropped away into inky blackness. Tiny flecks of dust drifted upward through the beam of her light, riding on a slow, warm updraft that reeked of dust, mortar, and rat droppings.

"Norman?"

No answer.

Her right foot had already found a horizontal framing member. There were plenty, spaced about two feet apart, perfect footholds for climbing down. Norman's footprints and handprints had already gone before her.

"Mr. Loman, I'm going to go down and find him. Maybe you should get us some help."

"Maybe you should wait!" he said, sounding quite nervous.

"Maybe he's hurt. Maybe he isn't breathing. There isn't time."

She saw his face disappear from the vent opening and turned away, lowering one foot, then the other, easing and sliding down the shaft from foothold to foothold. She still couldn't see the bottom.

ൟ

"The culprit is an African spotted wolf?" Sarah asked, studying the image on Algernon's computer screen.

Algernon fidgeted in his chair, drummed his knee, swiveled from side to side. "A *male* spotted wolf, to be exact." He shook his finger in Sarah's direction. "Every soda straw but one was occupied by a male. It's an old war tactic used in Africa, particularly Kenya: plant female pheromone on your enemy—give them a gift, an article of clothing, anything, but first confine it with some females to get the scent planted on it. Then put a male spider nearby so he's attracted by the pheromone. He crawls onto the victim, doesn't find the female he thought he'd find, he gets upset, he bites the victim. Victim goes crazy and eventually dies, and no one even knows it was the act of an enemy."

Sarah was stunned. "So somebody planted the spiders in the lockers, and the duffel bags, and the jacket, trapped in soda straws."

"And planted the pheromone on the victim. The male smells it, eats and claws his way out of the straw . . ."

"It's too perfect."

"Exactly. That's why we have such a terrible mistake here."

"The female."

"Exactly, exactly!" Now Algernon jumped up and pointed to the straw he'd dissected. "This straw had a *female* inside. The female doesn't get as upset as the male, so she usually doesn't bite, and that's why Blake Hornsby never showed any symptoms. BUT!" Algernon was too upset to stand still, so he paced, spun on his heels, paced some more. "Never, never, *never* turn a female spotted wolf loose in North America! She might mate with a brown recluse, and while the venom of the African spotted wolf is poisonous, it's nothing compared to the venom of the hybrid! Remember? The last two victims died within twenty-four hours, not several weeks! It's fair to say they were probably bitten by hybrids."

"Oh, Lord help us!"

"It gets worse, Sarah! Are you with me?"

"I'm with you."

"The hybrid breeds like crazy! It's like a cancer, like an invasion from another planet, it's, it's *unreal!* Once a brown recluse and an African spotted wolf find each other, you could have hundreds—NO! You'd have *thousands* of hybrids in a matter of days! Thousands of brown wolf hybrids! The Kenyan disaster!"

"Elisha . . . !" Sarah raced for the kitchen and found her hand-held radio. "NO! Oh, no!"

Algernon raced after her. "What, what, what?"

"This thing's been turned off all this time! Elisha may have tried to call me." She switched it on and called, "Elisha!" No answer. "Elisha, come in!"

ово

Elisha had reached the bottom of the shaft. It had emptied into a long, narrow space between a wall of the new building and a remaining wall of the old building, and her theory was right. There was space enough for her to crawl from behind Blake Hornsby's locker to behind Amy Warren and Crystal Sparks' lockers upstairs. If she could do it, obviously a tiny spider could do it.

And there were plenty in here. She could see their tiny dark shapes moving along the walls, scampering through the cracks, hanging from their webs. In fact, as she continued to look below, ahead, and above her, it became frighteningly clear that there were far *too many*. They were everywhere. The boards, the masonry, the dusty walls seemed alive with them.

She made sure her face shield was snapped securely shut. This was weird, so weird it was getting scary.

"Norman?" she called.

"Elisha!" her radio squawked.

The sound was so loud and sudden it made her jump. "Hello? Mom?"

"Where are you, honey?"

Elisha swallowed. "We might have an emergency, Mom. Norman went down the shaft first and disappeared. I'm in the shaft now, looking for him."

Apparently her mother had pressed the talk button but then paused to listen to someone else. Elisha could hear another voice in the background—it had to be Professor Wheeling—going absolutely nuts. "—near Blake's locker! The female has a nest back there. Get her out of there right now! She's going to . . ." She couldn't understand the rest. Finally her mother's voice came on. "Elisha? Listen to me. You're in serious danger where you are. You have to get out of there!"

"But what about Norman?"

"We'll get some help, don't worry. Just get out of there right now, do you hear me?"

Just looking around, Elisha was quite convinced. "Okay. I'm going back the way I came."

"Call me when you get out."

"Okay."

She turned quickly. A board snapped under her foot, she went off balance, put out the other foot to catch herself—

It broke open a hatchway and she fell through it, her skull smacking against the hatch frame. Stunned and limp, she tumbled through empty, black space, landed belly-down on a large, metal heating duct, slid off, fell, landed on another duct, rolled off, then tumbled down a slope of rubble to an old concrete floor where she finally came to rest, still and unconscious.

Her radio remained attached to her belt, but the line to her headset had pulled loose, so it was silent. The radio's tiny red power indicator light was the only thing visible in the total darkness—until something covered it.

11

DOLLARS AND
SCENTS

LGERNON WAS PACKING UP his gear, throwing everything back in the cases. "We've got to get down to the school right now. They have to close that place! They have to get everybody out!"

Sarah warned, "That may not be easy."

He looked at her, his crooked eyes now crazy with alarm. "Oh, there is no choice in this matter! What happened in Kenya could happen here!"

She grabbed his arm. "Algernon! What happened in Kenya?"

"You don't know?" Then he wagged his head and began correcting himself. "No, of course, she doesn't know, you dummy! You think everybody cares about bugs the way you do?"

She still had hold of his arm, and now she jerked it violently. "Algernon! *What happened in Kenya?*"

He scrambled to the Springfields' computer. "Do you have Internet access?"

"Answer my question!"

"I AM answering your question! Internet access, Sarah—oh, and pardon me for raising my voice!"

She tapped out the steps for going on-line.

While the computer chirped and warbled over the phone lines, Algernon looked at Sarah as directly as he could, his eyes wild, and gasped it out. "It happened in 1932. An American vessel loaded goods and fruit in Kenya, then sailed for America. Perfectly normal commerce. Happens all the time. But some spotted wolves got on board, hiding in the fruit, and . . ." He looked off into space as if viewing the whole story on an invisible movie screen. "And there were brown recluses aboard the ship. No one knows how many." He sniffed a little laugh and added, "Of course, all you'd need is *one.*"

The computer was on-line. He tapped out a Web site and hit the enter key.

As the first image downloaded, he continued, "The ship went off course, then totally adrift. It was missing for weeks, and wouldn't answer any radio calls. A Japanese freighter finally sighted it out in the middle of the Indian Ocean and pulled alongside." He looked into space again, staring at the images racing through his brain. "All the crew were dead—horribly dead. They'd torn the ship apart, destroyed every room, smashed all the equipment, savagely beaten and stabbed each other—and the ship was crawling with spiders."

The Web page was on-screen, some kind of technical page with links to various insects and their habitats. Algernon clicked a link, banged some keys, and found another image. "With *this* spider! The brown wolf hybrid."

Sarah thought the other images were gruesome, but they were tame compared to this one. This spider was large, covered with bristles, coal black with yellow stripes along its belly, with glistening rat's eyes—at least seven—and what looked like silvery tusks.

Algernon shook his head in wonder. "Just look at the fangs on that thing."

☙❧

Elijah took Mr. Maxwell through the front door and through the metal detector, and by now he was drawing enough stares from the students filling the halls that he felt stark naked. He could only hope this had all been cleared with Ms. Wyrthen and Officer Carrillo.

Plenty of kids wanted to greet Max and give him some pets, and of course, Max was more than happy to receive them.

But that's when it started. A girl came up, her hand extended. "Hi, nice doggie! How you doin'?"

Max didn't mind getting a pet, but he smelled something on her hand. Alerted, he looked at Elijah, fidgeting, whimpering.

The girl jerked her hand away. "Oh, does he bite?"

"No, not at all," Elijah answered. "But—"

A boy saw what happened and told the girl, "Hey, that's a drug-sniffing dog!"

That scared her. "Is he?"

Elijah tried to answer, "Well, yeah, but—"

"Good-bye." She turned away.

Max tried to follow her. Elijah held him back on his leash.

Then he sniffed a tall senior walking by and alerted again, sniffing at the young man's carry bag and whimpering.

The young man jerked his bag away. "Hey, what is this?"

Elijah was just as startled. "Uh, nothing. Max, are you—"

The guy was mad. "Well, I'm not carrying any drugs, so keep that dog away from me!"

The talk was spreading. Elijah could hear it as he and Max moved down the hall. "Drug dog!" "It's a drug-sniffing dog!" "Springfield's a *narc?*"

Talk about the Red Sea parting before Moses! The bodies in the hallway moved aside, ran ahead, made room, as if Max had an invisible bumper ten feet all around him.

But Max was acting crazy, whimpering, racing one direction and then another, his nose along the wall, then up against the lockers, then up against anyone who still came close enough. A cute little freshman girl walked by, smiled at Max, and said hello. He sniffed her handbag and alerted, looking at Elijah excitedly.

> But Max was acting crazy, whimpering, racing one direction and then another, his nose along the wall, then up against the lockers, then up against anyone who still came close enough.

"Max, are you sure?" Elijah asked.

Max only whimpered and nudged the girl's handbag again.

Someone called, "Look out! That's a drug-sniffing dog!"

The little girl was perplexed. "But . . . I don't use drugs."

Elijah gave Max a pet to calm him down. "Uh, sorry, I think he's a little confused."

She gave Max a friendly wave and walked on.

Max smelled something across the hall and tugged at his leash again. Then another student passed by and he lurched nose-first in that direction. He was getting too upset to handle.

Elijah had a terrible thought: What if he *isn't* confused?

∽

Marquardt was getting brash, as if he enjoyed upsetting this stranger in his office.

"You have to realize, kids like Norman Bloom attract this kind of treatment. Maybe it's nature's way of bringing us all up to par. Tod Kramer picked on him, Jim Boltz picked on him, Blake Hornsby picked on him . . ."

Nate glanced at the clock on the wall just above Marquardt's head. Soon the bell would ring and classes would start. The school would be filled with kids. Elijah had no doubt arrived with Max, and Nate hadn't even asked if Max could sniff out the locker room.

He saw something.

Marquardt was still talking. "There was Doug Anderson and—who was that other kid?—Baynes. Yeah, Leonard Baynes.

Craig Forbes, a few others. Hey, even *I* picked on him, if that's what you want to call it." He laughed to himself. "I've chewed him out quite a few times, but believe me, he'll live."

If the tiny dot had not descended across the white face of the wall clock, Nate probably would not have seen it. But Nate only needed a second look to discern the oval-shaped body and the outstretched, groping legs, the silvery, vertical web line, thinner than human hair, by which the spider was lowering itself directly toward Marquardt's head.

"So if you ask me—" Marquardt was saying.

"Excuse me," Nate said as he grabbed Marquardt by the arm and yanked him forward.

Marquardt cursed and jerked his arm loose, ready for a fight.

"I'm very sorry," Nate said, looking into Marquardt's face. Marquardt could see no fight in Nate's eyes and relaxed a little. Nate pointed. "Take a look."

Marquardt followed Nate's gaze just in time to see a thin, spindly, brownish-red spider alight on Marquardt's chair. It began scurrying around the chair in circles as if searching for something.

Nate spotted an empty water glass sitting on Marquardt's desk. He reached over, grabbed it, and placed it upside down over the spider, trapping it.

Marquardt sneered. "Oh, brother, you're going to get all upset over a little spider?"

"Just bear with me a second."

"Why, what's the matter?"

Nate looked up at the flat, rectangular light fixture above

Marquardt's chair. A broken strand of web line still dangled from it, waving in the moving air. The spider had come from up there. Nate climbed up on the desk.

"Hey!" Marquardt exclaimed, and then, seeing the serious, intense expression on Nate's face, said nothing more.

Nate peered into the narrow space between the fixture and the ceiling. There, amid the dust and dead bugs, lay a soda straw, the sugar plug half chewed and lying just to one side. He came within inches of touching it—

He could hear a frantic, rustling sound just above his head, like hundreds of tiny, crackling fires—like thousands of tiny claws *tick, tick, ticking* inside the ceiling.

All across the ceiling.

Behind the walls.

He got down from the desk, his eyes never leaving that corner of the room. He looked again at the tiny spider under the glass. "Mr. Marquardt, has Norman Bloom given you any money?"

Marquardt couldn't believe the question. *"What?"*

"Has Norman Bloom given you any money recently?"

The gym teacher was intrigued if not alarmed. "Yeah. Five dollars for a basket fee."

"Was it in paper dollar bills?"

Marquardt was already digging in his hip pocket. "Yeah. I've got 'em right here."

"Put them on the desk, please."

Apparently Nate's manner was serious enough to convince

Marquardt to comply. He pulled out five one-dollar bills and tossed them on the desk.

Then he stood back.

The spider under the glass became frantic, clawing at the sides of the glass, climbing the sides, falling, climbing again.

And it began to sound like there was a fire inside the ceiling.

Marquardt was becoming a believer. His voice had lost its gruffness when he asked, "What's going on? What is this?"

"Better stand back," was all Nate could say.

Something began to emerge from the cracks between the ceiling panels and where the ceiling met the walls: tiny black creatures scurrying in frantic, erratic patterns like ants on an upside-down anthill, so many that they dirtied the ceiling panels from white to gray to a coarse, boiling black. They dropped from the ceiling on web lines like storm troopers and flowed down the walls like thin black lava. They reached the top of the desk and raced toward the dollar bills. Within moments, the five bills were covered, alive and twitching like strips of bacon in a frying pan.

Nate and Marquardt were already backing toward the door.

"The dollar bills," said Nate. "The pheromone was on the dollar bills."

⚬⚬⚬

Sarah was frightened, truly frightened. "I've . . . I've never heard of this, this Kenyan thing."

"Oh, who has, other than bug nuts like me?" Algernon

clicked on some more links with the mouse. "Come on, come on . . ." The Web sites flashed by, the menus, the lists of further links. "It's here somewhere." He found it. "Here's an article about it. I never thought we'd be dealing with this . . . but then again, it's just so unthinkable!"

Sarah leaned down and studied the computer screen, scrolling down as she quickly scanned the fine print and technical details.

Algernon recapped the article. "The American and Japanese navies both converged on the scene and decided there was nothing else they could do but set fire to the ship with all the dead men—and the spiders—on board, and then sink it with artillery fire. Now Kenya and several other tropical countries have import and export restrictions to keep it from happening again." He stared at her. "Sarah? Sarah, what is it?"

She'd scrolled down to an old news photograph of the ill-fated ship with what looked like navy ships floating nearby. The photograph was vague and fuzzy, but the prow of the ship was close enough, big enough to make out the ship's name painted on its side.

The ship was named the *Abel Frye*.

⨉

Talk about the drug-sniffing dog was rippling up and down the halls. Some kids were running away, some were running to have a look. Mr. Maxwell just kept running in crazy circles as if being pulled by his nose.

Elijah jerked his collar, commanded him to sit, and took out a small vial. He uncorked it and let Max sniff it—again. "Okay, boy, now *this* is what we want. Sniff for *this,* okay?" It was a sample of the female pheromone, and Elijah was hoping to get Max redirected.

The commotion in the hall brought Officer Carrillo on the run, pounding around a corner with all his cop gear jangling on his belt. "All right, what's going on here?" The moment he saw Elijah and Max he pulled up short, his hands on his hips. "Oh, brother, now what?"

Max knew what to sniff for—and the first place he found it was on Officer Carrillo.

"Hey! What gives here?"

Elijah gave Max more leash and freedom to follow his nose. Max went to the wall again, sniffing the lockers, even jumping up and pawing them. A girl walked by. His nose went straight to her jacket and she jumped and squealed, "Hey!"

Max kept going, finding more of the scent. And more. And more.

"It's everywhere!" Elijah whispered in horror.

ॐ

Nate and Marquardt got out of the office and slammed the door behind them. Marquardt took off his jacket to block the crack under the door.

"No," said Nate. "Your jacket probably has the scent on it."

"Towels," said Marquardt, dashing for the showers. He returned with several towels and stuffed them under the door.

Through the window in the door they could see the spiders spreading all over the office, crawling over the furniture, along the shelves, up the filing cabinet, along the floor. They came at the door, directly for the towels stuffed under it.

Nate grimaced. "You handled those towels! Your hands have the scent on them!"

The very next look through the window proved Nate's point. The spiders were clustering on Marquardt's hat, his street shoes, his clipboard, the drawer handles—anything Marquardt had touched.

They were working their way into the towels under the door. The first few were coming through.

❧❧

The Holy Roller was rolling like a huge bus toward the school, with Algernon in the front passenger seat and Sarah at the wheel.

"By now there could be thousands of females," Algernon explained, his voice high-pitched with excitement. "They'll be flooding the school, leaving their scent everywhere, anywhere they like to hide—warm, dark places: lockers, clothing, back-packs, hair. From there, it can spread from surface to surface, hand to hand, hand to object. The males will follow, of course—and it doesn't take much to upset them."

Sarah had to concentrate on driving. She tossed her cell phone to Algernon. "Call Nate." She told him the number.

Nate grabbed his cell phone from his belt. "Sarah?"

"Nate, we've found out what spider we're dealing with and it's most likely in the building!"

Nate was just now pulling Marquardt out of the shower. The desperate gym teacher was trying to wash himself off, clothing and all. "There isn't time. We'll hose you off later." He spoke to Sarah. "Where are you?"

"Algernon and I are en route to the school right now. Nate, we may have to get everyone out of the school! We don't know where the spiders will crop up next."

Nate and Marquardt were heading for the locker-room door, dancing and hopping around spiders that were scurrying under their feet. "I take it the spiders are deadly?"

"Very deadly. And Algernon says there could be hundreds by now."

Nate looked over his shoulder and could see the locker-room floor darkening with the creatures. "Uh . . . copy that."

"Very deadly. And Algernon says there could be hundreds by now."

They burst through the door, into the hall. By now the halls were almost empty. The kids were settling into their homerooms for attendance and announcements.

"Right there!" Marquardt yelled, pointing.

Nate saw the fire alarm on the wall. He yanked it open and threw the switch. The fire alarms went off all over the building.

"Where are the kids?" Sarah cried.

Elijah came running down the hall, dragging Max by his leash, followed closely by Officer Carrillo. Max was fighting the leash every step of the way, obsessed with the pheromone scent coming from all directions.

"I've got Elijah. He's right here with Max."

"What's happening here?" Carrillo demanded.

The doors all along the hall burst open, and kids spilled into the halls for what they thought was a fire drill.

"Keep them out of this hall!" Nate told Carrillo.

"Other way!" Carrillo hollered at the approaching throng. "Don't use this hallway! Other way!"

The crowd turned the other way.

Marquardt joined Carrillo, directing traffic, blocking the hall. "Other way, other way, let's move!"

"Do you see Elisha?" Sarah asked over Nate's cell phone.

Nate bounded up a stairway as Elijah and Max followed. "I'm heading upstairs right now. Do you have her on the radio?"

"Nate, she went inside the wall."

"She *what?*"

"A friend of hers fell inside and she went down after him."

"What friend?"

"Norman. You know, that boy from biology class."

Nate stopped dead in his tracks and Elijah almost ran into him.

"Dad—?" Elijah just about asked.

Nate took the last few steps in one bound and made it to the second floor. Elijah and Max followed.

"Sarah, tell her to get out of there right now!" Nate shouted into the phone.

"I told her, but I haven't been able to raise her since then."

"Get us some help. Police, fire, emergency crews, the works."

"They're already on their way."

"We're upstairs, heading for that air vent."

"I'll keep trying to raise her."

∞

In the deep, cold darkness under the school, there was no light, no sight, and no sound—except for a strange hissing, rustling sound like sand blowing across the floor, the walls, everything.

Elisha heard nothing. She didn't stir.

∞

Nate could see the ladder up against the wall. He, Elijah, and Max had to weave between fire-drilling students to get there, and Max kept smelling more of the scent as kids rushed past him.

233

Mr. Loman was standing at the top of the ladder, holding a flashlight and looking worried. "Thank goodness! Your daughter's down there!"

"Down where?" Nate demanded. "I need to know exactly *where!*"

Mr. Loman only shook his head. "I don't know where this thing goes. I, I called the police, the fire department . . ."

Mr. Harrigan, the biology teacher, was at the base of the ladder, already studying the blueprints Elisha had left there. Nate came alongside. "What've you got?"

"The vent used to drop through both floors into the basement," Harrigan answered, leafing through the plans. "This cavity might still be there, the old furnace room."

"There has to be a way in there." Nate spoke into his cell phone. "Sarah, Elisha, and Norman may have fallen into the old furnace room, a cavity under the gym. Where are you?"

"We're just pulling up in front of the building. There are fire trucks coming up the street."

"Tell the firefighters that the spiders are concentrated in the north end of the building, around the gym, around Blake Hornsby's locker, and"—he hated to say it—"and under the building, maybe in the old furnace room. We're going to—"

"Good grief!" Mr. Loman exclaimed, backing hurriedly down the ladder. Spiders were coming out of the air vent. They began crawling down the wall, down the ladder.

"Dad!" Elijah cried. "Look out!"

Spiders were dropping out of the lockers below the air vent, only a few feet from where Nate and Mr. Harrigan were kneeling. Nate bolted from the floor. "Get back! Those things are poisonous!"

Loman, Harrigan, and Nate backed away. There were kids in the hall. They saw the black creatures scurrying over the face of the lockers and went nuts, screaming, running the other way.

"Don't run!" Nate cautioned. "Leave quickly and quietly—" He almost ran into Ms. Wyrthen.

"What is it, Mr. Springfield?" she asked. He didn't have to tell her. She saw several spiders at her feet, gasped, stomped on them, and moved right along with the others as they hurried down the hall, herding frightened students ahead of them. "Clear the building, clear the building!" A girl was trying to get into her locker. Ms. Wyrthen turned her away. "No time, sweetheart."

"My makeup bag's in there!"

"Let's take care of you first."

Ms. Wyrthen hurried ahead, arms spread, shepherding students toward a safe stairwell.

Nate had his cell phone in one hand and the plans in the other. He shook a spider off one page, stomped it dead, then continued up the hall with the others, studying the school's understructure. "Sarah?" he called into his phone.

ॐ

The Holy Roller lurched to a stop in front of the main entrance. Sarah and Algernon scrambled out as throngs of students filled the sidewalks and fire trucks roared to a halt at the curb. "We're out front."

"Sarah," came Nate's voice over her cell phone. "Spiders are overrunning the place. We're cut off. We can't reach Elisha from here."

That was a blow. Sarah's mind raced. "What about that passage under the building, the one that goes to the witches' chamber?"

"That's what I'm thinking. But Elijah may be the only one who can fit through that opening."

She heard Elijah's voice in the background.

"Hey, I'm ready!"

℆

Elisha's eyes jerked open.

She could see nothing. She was in the dark, on her side, feeling pain from her ribs, her shoulders, her limbs. Her head was throbbing and she vaguely remembered smacking it when she fell. She lifted a hand to her head, a simple, reflex move—

Every inch of her protective suit crackled like millions of tiny fires, like static electricity flowing over her. She froze. The sound, the *feeling,* subsided, but only a little. Slowly, cautiously, she raised her hand to her forehead and found the headlamp still in place. Either it was broken or the on-off switch got bumped. As she groped for the switch, something small and gritty crunched under her gloved fingers and her fingertips became slippery. She found the switch, knowing it might not work.

Click. It worked. A beam of light penetrated the darkness before her, but it was hard to see. Her face shield was dirty, soiled with dark blotches.

The blotches were moving.

Her breathing stopped. Dared she even draw a breath? She could smell them, hear them, see them on her face shield, only inches from her eyes. Some had gotten under her hood. Her chin tingled as they crawled over it. She moved her lips just enough to close them, and felt their little clawed legs shying away.

She tried one careful, slow breath through her nose, then another. She was living one breath at a time.

Oh, precious Lord, she prayed only in her mind, *don't let me die.*

12

CRAWLING
MINIONS

E VERYBODY OUT!" MARQUARDT hollered, waving his arms at any kids who even turned his direction. "Other way! Other way! Get out of this hall!"

He kept moving up the hall, soaking wet from the half shower he had taken, yelling and scaring everyone, making sure that not one person was left in the north end of the building. It was working. They were clearing out. Hopefully he was staying ahead of the spiders.

He felt a tiny sting on his left calf, like a mosquito bite. He reached down, swatted his calf, saw a spider cross the toe of his shoe and another go up inside his pant leg. He struck at them, swatted his pant leg, saw three more scurrying up his leg. He yelled, then cursed, then screamed.

☙❧

Out on the lawn, in the parking lot, on the ball field, on the front sidewalk, some kids were screaming, swatting, finding spiders in their clothing, their hair.

"The fire extinguishers!" Algernon shouted to the fire chief.

"The carbon dioxide will knock the insects out long enough to remove them."

Firemen fanned out among the crowds of students, dousing them in clouds of cold CO_2. Screams went up with every white cloud of the stuff.

Ms. Wyrthen found a bullhorn and called out instructions: "Do not panic. Teachers, get all the kids away from the building. Throw off all the backpacks, jackets, purses. Have every one of them check their clothing, hair, whatever, for spiders. That goes for everybody, on all sides of the building."

Then Algernon shouted above the uproar, "And if you can save any intact specimens, we'd appreciate it." He asked a police officer, "Would you have an empty jar anywhere?"

On the north side, Marquardt came running, then rolling out of the building, tumbling on the ground, swatting, groping, growling, tearing at his clothes.

Marquardt came running, then rolling out of the building, tumbling on the ground, swatting, groping, growling, tearing at his clothes.

WHOOOSHHH! Tom Gessner doused him with a fire extinguisher. Marquardt coughed and gasped, waving away the white cloud while Gessner brushed and swatted spiders off his body.

"Mr. Marquardt," he asked, "where are the Springfields?"

Marquardt was losing his mind. "That Bloom kid! It's Bloom! He's trying to kill me!"

"Bloom?"

Officer Carrillo came running up. "Norman Bloom. He's let loose a million spiders in the building." He immediately hollered at a throng of students milling about. "Get away from the building! Move around to the front! To the front! Go, go, go!"

Marquardt screamed, "Agotta medda blame for me, getcha man, onnit steady, help!"

Gessner thought for a fraction of a moment. "Where's Norman now?"

"I dunno," Carrillo answered, trying to hold Marquardt down. Marquardt was screaming, swatting at invisible monsters in the air over his head. "He and that Springfield girl are down under the building somewhere."

"The witches' chamber," Gessner thought aloud.

Carrillo sat on Marquardt's chest, trying to block Marquardt's wild, swinging hands. "Help me hold Marquardt down, will you?"

Gessner grabbed one flailing hand while Carrillo grabbed the other. Then he saw some firefighters coming around the building. "Medics! We need some medics over here!"

The firefighters ran over to help, and Tom Gessner leaped to his feet and started running toward the front of the building.

"Gessner!" Carrillo hollered. "Where are you going?"

"I've got to find Mr. Harrigan!"

പ്രൈ

As firefighters moved into the school to clear everyone out, Nate, Elijah, and Max came running around the school to the front.

"Sarah!" Nate hollered.

"Right here!" Sarah ran toward them, and they met beside a big red hook-and-ladder truck. "Nate, she isn't out here. No one's seen her. She won't answer my radio calls!"

"Then she's still down there. Algernon!"

Algernon hurried over and started talking without needing a question. "She has a chance, a very good chance. She's wearing a protective suit, correct?"

"Yes. Toxic hazard."

"Fine. Excellent. And as far as we know, she hasn't come in contact with any female pheromone." He noticed Max standing beside Elijah. "Yes, yes! Officer! Sir!" The police captain, a very busy guy with radios, weapons, and police gear hanging all over him, hurried over. "Captain, may I introduce the Springfields? This is Nate. Nate, this is—"

"What do you need?" the captain tried to ask politely.

"Just tell him!" said Nate.

"Oh, sorry, sorry," said Algernon. "Captain, take this dog and have it sniff every student and teacher for any trace of pheromone. Anyone with pheromone on them, set them apart. Quarantine them and then check them for spiders."

"Elijah," said Nate, "go with Max and get him oriented, then come back and get into your hazard suit."

Elijah and Max went with the captain as he shouted orders to his men, waving his arms, directing traffic, putting the plan into action.

"And bring me any intact specimens!" Algernon called after them.

"Elisha!" Sarah reminded Algernon.

"I'm thinking!" He let his mental gears grind a moment. "If she's unconscious, that could be to her advantage because she won't move and disturb the spiders. If she's conscious and frightened, well . . ."

"Well *what?*"

He shook his head in frustration. "We absolutely must find her! But we'll have to wade through spiders to do it. That's the hard part."

"Unless we can reach her through the witches' passage," said Nate. "And Elijah may be the only one small enough to fit through there."

෴

Elisha figured she could either lie there the rest of her life—which might not be long—or try to do something about her situation. If she moved slowly enough, perhaps the spiders wouldn't mind. She drew a long breath, gradually so as not to inhale any spiders happening by her mouth, and then did a slow sit-up. The spiders crackled and rustled over the surface of her protective suit, but didn't seem any more upset.

Now the rest of the room came within the beam of her head-lamp. The ceiling was high, the floor and walls concrete. This had to have been the original furnace room for the old building. The furnace was gone, but the massive heat ducts were still in place, looking like a giant octopus—or spider—inverted against the ceiling. Looking straight up, she could see the opening she'd fallen through, most likely an opening for a cold-air duct that wasn't there anymore. Somebody had patched it shut with a flimsy sheet of plywood that now hung loose by two bent nails. Far across the room, and high above the floor, was a metal door. The stairway that once led up to it was gone.

Across the room, against the wall and beneath the leggy fur-nace ducts, was an old workbench, the yellow paint peeling, the drawer knobs brown with rust. Atop the bench, in neat rows, were clear glass jars and cages of fine mesh. She'd seen jars and cages like these before—in the bio-chem supply room. They were used to hold smaller reptiles and insect specimens.

Norman Bloom used them all the time.

> ## Looking straight up, she could see the opening she'd fallen through.

"Norman?" she called softly. There was no answer. She called a little louder, "Norman, I know you're down here—"

Above her, the metal door opened with a shrill creak, and a faint, orange light streamed into the room. The spiders immediately flinched, began to scurry for cover. "Right here," came a voice.

"Norman." She tried to speak quietly, without moving. "Are you all right?"

He didn't sound all right. "No, I wouldn't say so."

"Norman. Please listen. You have to think this through now. If you can turn this around, you need to do it. A lot of innocent people are going to get hurt if you don't."

"I can't, Elisha. It's too late."

"Norman—"

"Don't move, Elisha! If the spiders get upset they'll bite you."

With the addition of more light, Elisha could see that the jars and cages were crawling with spiders. In one cage, spiders were crawling over, under, and around several dollar bills. Her heart sank. "I take it those are females?"

"That's right. Squirting pheromone all over those dollar bills, trying to attract males—which they've done."

"Norman." She swallowed, fear and sorrow tightening her throat. "I'm sure you didn't intend to kill anybody. You're better than that."

After a difficult, silent moment, he answered, "I'm the one who brought in the spiders, Elisha. The African spotted wolves. I didn't think there would be any brown recluses around here.

They're only supposed to live in the southern and central United States. Looks like I was wrong."

"Brown recluses?"

"It's a poisonous spider that can mate with an African spotted wolf, if it gets the chance. And it looks like it did. I took all kinds of precautions: separate males and females, sealed cages, repellents. The wolves were doing great, doing just what I wanted them to do. But now . . . looks like the two species have mated with each other—just like they did aboard the *Abel Frye*."

"The *Abel Frye?*"

"A merchant ship carrying cargo out of Kenya. I found out about it on the Internet. It was overrun with spiders and the crew all killed each other. The navy had to sink it. It was such a great story I named the ghost after that ship."

"*You* named the ghost?"

He nodded. "It was perfect. I gave the school legend a new name, and *bam!*—I had my very own ghost of death and destruction. I got people believing, didn't I? Everybody thought the *ghost* was making people crazy. Even poor Ian." He peered down through the opening at the crawling sea of spiders. "But I wasn't planning on this." He watched for a moment, marveling. "Then again, maybe I wanted it to happen. It would have been easy. All

 "The wolves were doing great, doing just what I wanted them to do."

I had to do was find a brown recluse. Just one. I could have slipped it into a cage of females and *bam!*—this whole school would have gone down just like the ship, gone down with everybody on it."

"But you *didn't* want this to happen!"

"It happened, Elisha. That's all that matters now. I made a mistake somewhere. A female got out. I probably put her in one of the soda straws—the males and females look alike at that age."

Elisha had to remind herself not to move, not to react as she felt the horror creeping through her. "But . . . you put Tricanol in the sugar plugs, right? That had to be a controlling device."

"It was supposed to be. It's a slow-acting insecticide they put in wood preservatives and paints. Once the spider eats it, he lives a day or so, just long enough to bite somebody, but not bite everybody."

"So . . . that's what I mean. You never wanted to kill anybody."

"A lot of good that does me now. You can see what happened. The hybrids are everywhere. They've chewed their way into my cages, they've bred with my African wolves, they're breeding with

Elisha had to remind herself not to move, not to react as she felt the horror creeping through her.

each other. I imagine there are even more brown recluses getting into the act by now. I was hoping I could sneak the cages out of here before you found them, but now, here you are, and here the spiders are, all over you, all over everything. It's out of my hands. I have to go, Elisha."

"Norman! Please, you don't have to leave things this way! Norman!"

His voice trembled. "I'm sorry, Elisha. I really did like you."

ɘⓍɕ

More emergency vehicles rolled up in front of the school, lights flashing, sirens wailing. Paramedics, doctors, and nurses hopped out, unloading their medical kits. Algernon directed them to the quarantine area the police had set up. "Look for symptoms! Screaming, scratching, clawing, irrational fear of everything!"

They hesitated. From where they stood, screaming, scratching, clawing, and irrational fear seemed to be universal. The school was surrounded by pure bedlam, and now the police were burdened with keeping the local neighbors, as well as distraught parents, out of the area.

Then Officer Carrillo strode up. "Well? You heard the man! Let's move! You two, over there, and you—yeah, *you*—follow me! You got any blankets in that truck?"

As Carrillo took control of things—"And somebody bring a stretcher! We've got a nutty gym teacher around the back!"— Algernon hopped into one of the aid cars, got on the radio, and called the hospital. "Poison control, stat. Yes, hello ma'am. Well, I'm fine, thank you, and how about yourself? Listen, we have a case of spider bite here and we'll need some antitoxin. Do you have any AT490? Baylor-Schrift came out with a great product this year . . ."

Ms. Wyrthen and several teachers kept working through the clusters of distraught students, helping, soliciting help, inspecting, separating. "Okay, you're clean, step over there." "Stretch that rope between the trees, that's it. Now all of you, stay on that side of the rope!" "Don't worry, dear. You're going to be fine." "Yes, your folks are right over there, see? Wave so they can see you."

ထ

Nate pulled a protective suit from a storage hold of the Holy Roller and began putting it on, attaching another headset radio to his belt.

Sarah and two firefighters in smoke gear went over the building plans. Sarah showed the firefighters the old foundation lines and the location of the witches' passage under the building. "You may have to break some concrete, but if you can get under there, there might be a connection somewhere between that room and the old furnace room."

"Let's do it," said a burly firefighter, grabbing a sledgehammer from the fire truck.

"Ready, gentlemen?" said Nate. They joined him on the run,

and Sarah followed. "Elijah!" Nate called over his shoulder, "Get your suit on and meet us in back!"

"Got it!" Elijah responded, handing Max's leash over to Officer Carrillo.

Algernon saw them going. "Wait! You can't just go in there!" They didn't hear him. He asked the lady on the radio, "Listen, we need a big-time, industrial-strength exterminator out at the Baker High School right away." He winced at whatever she told him, then called out to no one in particular, "Does anyone have a copy of the Yellow Pages? Anyone at all?" He asked a fireman running by, "Would you happen to have a can of Raid?"

ॐ

"Norman. *Please.* You *can't* leave me here."

Norman lingered in the doorway like a frightened deer, ready to bolt at any moment. "Elisha, you know everything. I can't help you and survive. I have to get away."

"No, Norman. You have to stay here and face it and tell everyone why. I think they'll understand."

"Oh, don't insult my intelligence!"

"Just tell them—"

"They don't *care,* Elisha! It's not a big deal, don't you know that? Drugs are a big deal, guns are a big deal, but not this! I'm a *wimp,* Elisha, and out there, it's survival of the fittest, natural selection, only the strong survive. Well, okay, I found a way to survive. I found one way to be able to come to school and get an education without being beat up, laughed at, pushed around, and stolen from. If all those parents and teachers out there don't like it, well, they only have themselves to blame—but I know they're going to blame *me*. This whole thing's going to be *my* fault, not theirs! Anyway, good-bye."

"Norman! Please! You'll only make things worse for yourself!"

"Remember not to move, Elisha. If you move, they'll bite you."

Norman disappeared from the doorway. The door swung closed with another shrill creak and a metallic thud, leaving Elisha in the dark except for her headlamp.

She reached carefully, ever so slowly—the spiders scurried over her hand, all over the radio—and plugged her headset cord back into the radio on her belt. By God's grace, the headset was still situated on her head. "Mom . . . ," she said weakly, afraid even to move her lips.

෫෮෯

Sarah, running alongside Nate and two firefighters, grabbed her radio. "Elisha!" She shouted to the others, "I've got her!" then said into the radio, "Where are you?"

෫෮෯

Elisha sat still, watching the spiders crawl across her face shield as she answered, "Under the building, the old furnace room.

Norman had a lab down here. He was raising spiders—and they're loose."

"Are you all right?"

Her eyes moved from side to side, watching the spider traffic as she said, "So far."

"Is Norman down there?"

"No. He came to say good-bye, but he left me here. He looked in through a doorway in the wall a story above me, but there aren't any stairs. I can't reach it without a ladder."

"Elisha, we're coming to get you out."

"There has to be another way in and out of here, something Norman knows about. I can't see it from here."

"We'll find it. But be careful to stay away from the spiders! They're deadly poisonous! Do you copy?"

There may have been one clinging to her microphone as she spoke into it. "Yes, Mom. I copy."

꩜

Sarah stayed on the radio. "Elijah? Are you there?"

Elijah was pulling on a protective suit from the Holy Roller. He'd already grabbed another radio and had the headset in place. "Yes, Mom. I heard what she said."

"Tell the police. We have to find Norman."

Officer Carrillo was running by. Elijah called him, "Officer Carrillo!"

The moment Carrillo got the word from Elijah, he handed

Max to another officer and went on the prowl, chattering into his radio as he began circling the building. "Be on the lookout: Suspect is thin, with glasses, probably has pimples, isn't armed but is probably dangerous . . ."

He passed Mr. Harrigan coming the other way. Harrigan asked Elijah, "What's this about Norman?"

"Elisha saw him. He stuck his head in the door of the old furnace room and told her good-bye, and then he left her there. We have to find him. If he could just leave Elisha down there, then he must know a way out—which would be a way *in*."

"He'll know more than that," said Harrigan, looking around thoughtfully. "Let me try a hunch."

And with that, he ran toward the school.

No one noticed. All around Elijah were running, shouting, noise, fear, commotion. Medics were running every which way, cops were herding hysterical kids, Max was sniffing everybody brought close to him. Ms. Wyrthen was right in the thick of it, using the bullhorn to maintain order, dashing about like a border collie as she separated kids who were clean from kids who needed to be quarantined.

It looked like the quarantine area might work. The students were lining up so Max could sniff them. Any student tainted with pheromone was getting set apart and checked over. The doctors and nurses were finding spiders, but now they had several cans of Raid from the local hardware store, and they were using it.

Oh, brother! Here came a team of medics carrying Mr. Marquardt on a stretcher, heading toward an ambulance. He was squirming and struggling the whole way, hollering like a wildcat and trying to bite anyone within reach. Elijah couldn't help staring as he zipped up the front of his suit and cinched up the gloves.

Then a voice behind him said, "Cool."

It was Ian Snyder.

"Ian!" Elijah whispered, knowing Ian was still a fugitive.

Ian must have known it, too. His hair was cut, all his facial jewelry was gone, he was wearing a drooping hat, and—most stunning of all—he was dressed in designer jeans and a Chicago Bulls tee shirt. "So old Marquardt finally got cut down to size. You gotta love it."

Elijah looked under the hat to catch Ian's eyes directly. "Ian. It was spiders. Norman Bloom was planting poisonous spiders in people's lockers and bags and coats. I don't know how he knew which kids you were cursing, but—"

"He was one of us."

Elijah did a double take. "Excuse me?"

"Don't you get it? He's—he *was*—a witch. We had the same enemies. He was with us when we cursed those people."

Elijah was incredulous. *"Norman?"*

Ian shrugged. "Why not?"

Elijah considered that and had to nod in agreement.

"But yeah, I see it," said Ian. "We put a curse on people, and then Norman sneaked off and planted the spiders." He wagged his head in wonder. "So there never was a ghost."

"No. People were hallucinating. The poison does that."

Ian chuckled at himself, obviously feeling foolish. "Norman was with us at the séance when Abel Frye told us his name. He must have *made* the Ouija board spell it. And he probably made the Ouija board tell us what Abel Frye looked like, too."

"Ian. Please don't hate him. You have enough problems without adding that."

Ian wagged his head resignedly. "I don't hate him. I *envy* him, maybe. The guy's clever. He had all of us going. But I guess that doesn't matter much anymore."

"Well listen . . ." Elijah tucked his protective hood under his arm. "Elisha's trapped under the school and we have to get her out."

Ian went pale. "You gotta be kidding."

Elijah came clean. "Ian, I have a confession to make."

"You're a team of investigators."

Elijah stopped and looked at him. "I guess it's kind of obvious by now, isn't it?"

Ian gave a playful smirk. "Oh, no. A lot of high school kids have drug-sniffing dogs, motor homes, bug-proof suits, and dads who aren't really janitors."

Elijah twisted his lip in acknowledgment. "Well. I'm confessing it anyway. We know about that ritual chamber you have under the school. I'm sorry I didn't tell you, but we were in there, we know about it. We're going to have to go in that way to get Elisha—"

"It isn't there anymore."

Elijah stared at him. "What do you mean?"

"It isn't there anymore. I took all that stuff out and burned it. It's history."

"But the passageway—"

"I caved it in!"

That hit Elijah like a spear through the heart.

❧

Mr. Harrigan had to try two different routes employing three different stairways to avoid spiders and reach his classroom. With advancing spiders only a few doors down the hall, he finally burst into the room, almost knocking over a model of a human skeleton, and rounded the corner into the supply room.

Tom Gessner was already there. "Mr. Harrigan! I was looking all over for you!"

And there, sitting next to the rabbit, snake, and mice cages, was Norman Bloom, his head in his hands, weeping.

Harrigan was impressed. He told Gessner, "Looks like you and I had the same idea."

Gessner only shrugged. "Well, I was actually trying to find you because I thought you could help me find Norman. This was the last place I looked."

Mr. Harrigan approached Norman and put his hand on the boy's shoulder. "This has always been Norman's little world back here, the one place where he feels safe. Am I right, Norman?"

Norman didn't look up but only said, "Just leave me here. Please."

"Can't do it, Norman," said Mr. Gessner.

"The spiders are moving up the hall," said Harrigan. "We have to get you out of here."

"You should let them kill me," the boy replied.

Mr. Harrigan stooped low and made eye contact with him. "Norman. I'll come right out and say it: We should have been looking. We should have been there for you. The stuff you've gone through shouldn't have happened and we're partly to blame. But we're here for you now, and we're not going to leave you here."

Norman looked away. "It's too late—"

Mr. Harrigan grabbed his chin and turned his head forward again. "Norman. You left somebody under the building, and I think you know what it's going to take to save her life. Now yes, we owe you, but you owe her." Norman's eyes dropped. Mr. Harrigan followed and made even closer eye contact. "You owe Elisha, a gal who was a friend to you. What's it going to be, Norman?"

Norman looked back at Mr. Harrigan for a moment, then nodded. "I was scared."

"But you're still here. I think you want to do the right thing, so come on. Here's your chance."

He wiped his eyes, sniffed, and then said, "I need my coat. It's right over there."

"We have to hurry."

ॐ

"NO!" said Nate. "NO, NO, NO!"

"Elisha!" Sarah called. "Are you still there?"

A faint voice came back. "Still here. Where are you?"

She couldn't give an encouraging answer. She, Nate, and the firefighters had reached the hole that led to the passageway, but stones and rubble now blocked the old opening. They wouldn't be going in this way.

"Dad!" Elijah hollered, running through the bushes with Ian right behind him. "Ian knows another way inside!"

Nate and Sarah took only a split second to adjust to Ian's new appearance, and then Nate said, "Lead on."

Ian led them out of the brush and then farther around the building to an old Dumpster. He pushed on the Dumpster; they all helped, and the Dumpster rolled aside to reveal a sheet of plywood covering an opening in the concrete slab. To anyone who didn't know better, the plywood appeared to cover a grease pit and nothing more. But when they lifted it aside, they found a concrete stairway underneath.

"This wasn't on the plans!" Nate remarked.

"Ah, I'll bet this is a Barton!" said the fireman named Al.

"A Barton?"

"Barton was the old building inspector," said the fireman named Larry. "He probably made the contractors put this in after the building was almost finished."

Al the fireman laughed. "It's got to be a fire exit for the old basement. Barton was always requiring extra holes and tunnels and vents."

"I think the county fired him before the town decided to hang him," Larry added.

The two firefighters shared a laugh.

"Well, God bless him!" Nate countered.

"Got that right."

"Come on," said Ian. "I'll show you what I can." He started down the stairs and the others followed.

❧

Algernon was on the cell phone in the Holy Roller, the Yellow Pages open in front of him. "Yes, that's right. Tricanol. It's an insecticide." He stuck a finger in his ear to block out the ambulance sirens. "Check your lawn and garden department, and if they don't have it, check the paint department, particularly the wood preservatives. If you have it, bring it." He hung up, somewhat satisfied, then picked up a glass jar containing live specimens, crawling and scratching against the glass. "Ah, me. Your beauty is in your terror." He looked toward the school. "Be careful down there."

❧

Elisha rose slowly, ever so slowly, to her feet. There had to be a way out of here. She scanned the room, rotating slowly like a lighthouse. The spiders didn't seem to like it. She stopped moving until they calmed down. The door Norman had looked through wasn't an option; it was unreachable. Were there any other doorways or exits? It was so dark it was hard to tell without moving her light around, which meant she had to move her head.

She felt a tickle on her neck, and fear jolted up her spine.

ॐ

Ian and Elijah led the way through a tunnel up to a steel door. The lock on the door had been broken long before and the door swung open easily. On the other side was a room of the old basement, cluttered with fallen steel and concrete.

Since he was wearing a protective suit, Elijah went in first, shining his light in every direction, looking for spiders. Carefully, they continued into the weird maze of rubble and scrap, ducking, sometimes crawling, eyes wide open for any dark spots or blotches that might move.

"See through there?" Ian asked, pointing down a narrow space between slabs of fallen concrete. "That's the way to the ritual chamber."

"So how do we get to the furnace room?"

"I don't know."

Elijah stopped and looked at him. "You don't know?"

Ian shrugged. "I've got a confession, too."

"Yeah?"

"I knew about the old stairway under the Dumpster, but I don't know where this goes."

"You don't—!"

"I've only used this passage to get to the ritual chamber. I haven't explored the rest of it."

Nate came up behind them, followed by the firefighters. "Problem?"

"Not yet," said Elijah.

They got moving again.

໕ໆ

Elisha drew short little gasps of air, each one quavering with fear as she felt a tingle here, a rustle there, a tickle moving across her skin. They'd crawled up under her hood, she didn't know how many. Should she move? Should she stand still? A trickle of sweat ran down from her forehead, down her cheek. Her face shield was fogging up.

"Dear Jesus, please help me," she prayed, barely moving her lips.

Wait. She heard something. Movement, some thumping and scraping. Voices muffled by earth, walls, and concrete.

She spoke into her radio. "Mom? I think I hear something."

"Yes, honey," her mom came back. "Your dad and brother are on their way in. They have some firemen with them—and Ian Snyder, too."

Then she heard a muffled voice from above. "Elisha! Elisha!" Her dad.

She decided she would answer. She didn't know how loudly, but there was no way on earth she would remain silent. "Hello!"

It was a weak little sound. She could hardly hear it herself. "Hello!" The spiders tensed. She could feel their legs gripping her skin. *I'm going to faint.*

"Elisha!" Her mother's voice came to her over her radio.

She drew a breath and answered. "They're getting close, Mom. I can hear them above me."

Then her dad came over the radio. "Call out to us, honey. Let us know where you are."

She called out *almost* loudly. "I'm in here!"

She heard the voices somewhere above, muted, but growing stronger. "I heard her." "Over this way." "Look out! There goes one!"

This time her brother called, "Elisha!"

She called out boldly. "Help! I'm in here!"

Someone rattled the door above, the one Norman had used. It didn't open. "Okay, stand back," a stranger said.

"No!" she cried. "Don't make a disturbance!"

BANG! CRUNCH! The door flew open from the blow of a sledgehammer, slammed into the wall, then fell from its hinges and into the room. Spiders went scurrying outward as from an explosion. An old nail pinged off Elisha's head and she flinched.

She felt a bite on her shoulder and screamed.

Another bite, on her neck.

A warm feeling began to radiate through her skin. The poison moving.

13

VERITAS

NOW THE BEAMS from several flashlights began to sweep about the room, and that upset the spiders even more. There was no time to worry about care and caution. Elisha called out desperately, "Please get me out of here! The spiders are biting me!"

❧

From above, they could see her standing in the center of the room, one lone, frightened figure in a sea of swirling black, cowering, shaking, a lone beam from her headlamp creating a yellow cone in front of her.

The firemen backed away, chilled by the sight.

"It's going to take a rope from here," said Al.

"But . . . what are we going to do about the spiders?" asked Larry.

Nate countered, "Just get the rope down there!"

Larry had a rope clipped to his belt. He unclipped it and got ready to toss it down.

Nate called through the doorway, "Elisha! Can you make it to the wall? We're going to throw a rope down."

She didn't move from where she stood. She was trembling.

"Elisha!"

"Daddy . . . ," she muttered in a dopey voice, "wha'd you say? I can't hear you."

"We're losing her," he whispered. "Lower the rope. I'll go down after her."

Larry held one end of the rope and tossed the rest through the doorway.

"Look out!" Elijah cried, stomping on some spiders coming through the opening.

Al brandished a can of Raid and saturated the area around the opening, clearing it for the moment.

"Awww!" Spiders were scurrying up the rope toward Larry's hands. In a panic, he let go.

His end of the rope fell through the doorway and into the darkness.

"No! NO!" Nate cried.

Ian backed away to a safe distance—and saw another beam of light moving toward them through the dark maze. "Hey! Somebody's coming!"

"Nate," came Sarah over the radio. "Tom Gessner and Mr. Harrigan are here with me. They brought Norman."

Nate was looking at his daughter, surrounded and covered by black spiders, and it took him a moment to check his anger and respond. "I don't suppose Norman has any help he can offer?"

"He knows another way down there. He's on his way right now."

"It's Norman!" Ian exclaimed as Norman Bloom came through the clutter, wearing his old jacket and carrying a flashlight.

Nate's eyes burned through his face shield. "Young man, do you have any usable suggestions?"

Norman was plainly afraid and intimidated, but he replied, "There's another way down there. I'll get her out."

"*I* can do that," said Nate.

Norman stepped forward, his voice trembling but bold. "Sir, you have to let me do it. The spiders won't bother me."

Everyone stared at him. He had no protective clothing. He was just a skinny kid in jeans, tennis shoes, and an old jacket.

"That's my daughter down there," Nate seethed.

"They're *my* spiders—sir!"

Nate weighed that for only a moment, then backed off. "All right. But hurry. She's been bitten and she's fading." Norman turned toward a black void between two fallen concrete slabs, and disappeared as if the void had swallowed him up.

"Can you get us another rope?" Nate asked Larry.

The fireman named Larry turned and headed out immediately.

"Elisha, hang on! Norman's on his way down there."

"We hope," said Ian. They looked back at him. "I trusted him, and look where that got me."

They heard Elisha's faint voice from below. "Daddy . . . I can't stand up . . ."

They shone their lights into the room. The small, orange-clad girl far below was teetering, weakening. Her protective suit was alive with dark little shadows.

Nate couldn't linger another moment. He called into his radio, "Where's that rope?"

"On the way," came Sarah's voice.

"Look!" said Al. "Will you look at that!"

A dim light appeared in the far corner of the furnace room. There was a metallic grating sound. A piece of fallen furnace duct rumbled aside, and Norman Bloom, a vague shadow in the dark, emerged from a passage behind it. Immediately, the spiders shied away from his feet like a wave receding from the shore, leaving a circle of bare concrete around him. He started inching his way toward the center of the room, toward Elisha. The circle of clear concrete moved along the floor with him, the spiders always maintaining an even distance.

Tom Gessner's voice came over the radio. "Mr. Springfield. Is Norman there? Did he make it through?"

Nate was transfixed by the sight below him. "He's here, Mr. Gessner."

"Is he of any help?"

Nate continued to watch as Norman kept moving slowly, the bare floor around him resembling a dim spotlight that followed him inch by inch. "He's helping, Mr. Gessner. He's definitely helping."

Norman kept moving slowly, giving the spiders time to retreat. "Try to keep still, Elisha." He called to the men above, "Please put out those lights. You're upsetting the spiders."

"Better do it," said Nate.

They extinguished their lights, and the nether world under the school fell into eerie, cavelike blackness. Below them, the old furnace room became a deep, soot-black well with only two lights visible: the light in Norman's hand illuminating Elisha, and the light from Elisha's headlamp, the beam wavering, sinking as she continued to weaken. Norman kept moving slowly, steadily, drawing closer to her, the spider-free circle moving with him, until its boundary crossed Elisha's feet.

$$\infty$$

Elisha began to whimper. She couldn't help it. The whole room seemed to be closing in on her, about to crush her. She felt the floor rocking like a ship in rough weather. She could only breathe in quick, little gasps.

"Hold still," said Norman. "I'm going to get you out of here."

She tried to hold still, but her image of Norman was getting fuzzy, unstable, and the closer he got, the more afraid she felt. *It's the poison,* she kept telling herself. *Hold still.* The spiders were reacting to Norman's approach. She could feel them scurrying over her skin, trying to find a way out of her clothing. Two shot out from under her hood and dropped on web lines from her shoulders to the floor. Those on the outside raced down her legs and hurried across the floor, vanishing in the darkness beyond the flashlights.

"Ohhh . . . help me . . ." The room began to move crazily. The ductwork above their heads came alive, pulsing and flexing like huge aluminum pythons.

She was afraid. Afraid!

Don't believe it! she told herself. *Don't give in!* "I'm not afraid," she tried to say, but it came out, "I no fear to me." A hand grabbed her arm and she tried to jerk away. "NO! It's no me in the manner, me nothing nothing!"

"Come this way," came a voice.

She looked and saw a face. Norman's face? It looked so strange, so dead and white . . .

"Go with him," came the voice of her father, but even his voice sounded evil.

" 'sokay, Elisha," came a slow, garbled voice that could have been her brother's.

"No . . . ," she cried, and her own voice sounded so slow, so far away . . .

The face before her, once Norman's, wavered, decayed. Now she saw a rotting skull, a broken and crooked neck, a hawk on a bony shoulder.

Abel Frye! He was pulling her into hell!

She lashed out at him, struck at him. Her arms moved slowly, a blur before her eyes. They may have contacted something, she didn't know. She thought she screamed, thought she may have tried pulling away, but everything slowed down, slowed down, faded away, went out of focus . . .

Blackness. Silence. Sleep.

ॐ

"Elisha!" Nate cried out as he saw his daughter's body go limp. Larry returned with another rope and threw it through the doorway. Nate grabbed it and was about to climb down when Al took hold of his arm.

"Easy," said the fireman. "He's got her. He's got her."

Norman held her up, his arms wrapped around her. Her head drooped, her headlamp shone downward. In its beam, they could see spiders dropping from her body, bouncing on the concrete like little raindrops, then scurrying away into the inky blackness.

"Norman," said Elijah, "what can we do to help?"

"Nothing," he replied. "Just give me time. I'll get there."

He held Elisha tightly, slowly walking back to the hidden passage in the corner as the spiders maintained the empty circle around them. Elisha's feet dragged along the floor.

"Mr. Springfield," came Tom Gessner's voice over the radio, "what's happening?"

Nate could hardly draw a breath to speak. "Norman has Elisha. He's bringing her out."

"We have paramedics standing by."

Sarah's voice came over the radio. "Nate, is she all right?"

"She's . . ." He couldn't answer. "Pray, Sarah. Pray."

ॐ

Paramedics scrambled down the secret stairway to meet them halfway. Within minutes, they emerged with Elisha's limp, pale body, her protective hood removed and an oxygen mask clamped over her face. Nate, the firefighters, Elijah, and Ian stepped out into the daylight right behind them.

"Algernon!" Sarah cried as the paramedics lowered Elisha onto a stretcher.

Algernon Wheeling quickly examined her face and neck. "Yes, several bites." He prepared a syringe as they cut away her protective suit. "This is AT490. I would say she needs a double dose. Administer this, please, and quickly."

A paramedic took the needle and jabbed it into her arm. "Okay, let's get her to the hospital."

They grabbed up the stretcher and raced to a waiting ambulance, the Springfields and Algernon Wheeling running after.

Norman and Ian went nowhere. Carrillo and another officer had already grabbed them, and now they brandished their handcuffs.

"Wait," said Mr. Harrigan, stepping in. "This isn't necessary."

"Put them in our custody," said Tom Gessner. "We can work something out, get them some counseling . . ."

Carrillo clamped the cuffs on. "Take it up with the judge, fellas. I'm hauling these punks in."

Tom Gessner put a hand on Carrillo's shoulder. "Then let us ride along. Come on, Dan. Please."

Carrillo considered the request, eye to eye with Gessner's kind gaze. "Okay, Tom. But we'd better get going before I change my mind."

⚬⚬

"I think she's waking up."

It was the first sound she recognized as a voice. She'd been listening to garbled sounds for what seemed like hours. She moved and became aware of her body. She could feel her hands brushing across bedsheets, feel the pressure of a pillow against her head.

Then she felt a hand on hers. "Elisha? Wake up, sweetheart." Mom's voice.

She opened her eyes. They rolled about lazily for a moment, trying to focus on something, and finally, after a few blinks, she recognized her family, standing around her bed. There was Mom, Dad, and Elijah. And there was Professor Wheeling. They were all grinning at her, then grinning at each other, looking so happy they looked silly.

A line from an old movie came to her and she managed to at least mumble it. "Oh, Auntie Em, there's no place like home!"

And they all laughed. She broke into a weak smile herself.

Professor Wheeling straightened up, looking very happy with himself. "Good ol' AT490! Good call, Wheeling, good call!"

Elisha made a puzzled face. "What's he talking about?"

Her dad explained, "The antidote for the spider venom. The medics gave you a double dose, and then the doctors had to give you an additional dose every day for a week, but it worked."

"Sweetheart," said Professor Wheeling, "you sustained over fifty bites. That would have been enough venom to kill at least that many people."

That alarmed her. "Am I all right?"

He was quick to reassure her, "Oh, yes, yes, absolutely! As a matter of fact, your own body has probably begun its own immunity program by now. I would be willing to wager that spider bites will no longer be a problem for you—uh, I wouldn't press my luck, of course . . ."

"Of course!" she said, recalling how it felt to have hundreds of spiders crawling all over her. "But . . . I've been out for a week?"

Her mother nodded, a grim kind of smile on her face. "We almost lost you."

Oh. There was Dr. Stuart, stepping around her family to get to her. Only now did she become aware that she was in the hospital!

Dr. Stuart took her pulse, then held a light to her eyes. "Look here." He waved the light back and forth—it made her want to blink—and then he put it in his shirt pocket and smiled. "I would say she's with us again."

"Praise God!" said Dad.

"Welcome back, sis," said Elijah.

She vaguely recalled the last thing she could remember—and then regretted remembering it. "I—I saw Abel Frye. He was standing right there in front of me. It was terrible."

"Now you know what the other kids went through," said Dr. Stuart. "They'd all heard the rumors and legends about Abel Frye and seen Crystal Sparks' painting of him, just as you did. All it took was the spider's venom to turn the legends into a frightening hallucination, their worst fears brought to life before their eyes."

"I—I saw Abel Frye."

"No wonder they were so scared! But . . . it was Norman, wasn't it? He came back to help me."

They nodded.

"What happened?"

They all looked at Professor Wheeling, so he answered. "Norman had also isolated a male pheromone, one the male uses to mark his territory and warn off other spiders. He applied it to the old jacket he was wearing, and that's how he managed to work around the spiders without being endangered by them—and it's how he managed to get you out of the old furnace room. The spiders all fled from the scent on his jacket."

"He saved my life."

"He certainly did," said Sarah.

"But . . ." Her heart sank. "There are the others. Amy and Crystal . . . the boys . . . What's going to happen to him?"

Nate betrayed a hint of a smile as he said, "Well, Officer Carrillo arrested him and Ian Snyder."

"They're going to go to prison, aren't they?"

Nate gave a half nod. "That's a real possibility. Some pretty terrible things have happened. Most of it was Norman's doing, but Ian could be charged as an accessory."

She looked away for a moment, feeling a wave of sadness. "I feel sorry for them. I mean, I'm not trying to say they're innocent, but if people only knew what they've been through!"

"I know Ian has a story to tell," said Elijah.

"And so does Norman! They just need someone to listen."

"Well," said Nate, "there is one ray of hope. Mr. Gessner and

Mr. Harrigan went to the judge and told him about a particular mentor program that seems to be working quite well in Montague, Oregon."

That brought a smile to her face. "You're kidding! You told them about that?"

Her dad nodded. "I made some calls. The police department and prosecutor's office in Montague sent some of their people up to help the town of Baker set up a similar program here—with Norman and Ian being the first participants. Ms. Wyrthen's all for it, the parents are asking for help, and Tom Gessner and Mr. Harrigan have volunteered to be mentors."

"That's great!"

Nate was still cautious. "We'll see. It's all probationary, and the judge has drawn some pretty tight boundaries."

"Ian will make it work," said Elijah. "He just needs to see that there's some love somewhere in this world, somebody willing to be a friend. *I'm* going to stick by him, that's for sure."

"Same goes for Norman," said Elisha.

"And with Gessner and Harrigan on board, it does look promising," Sarah replied.

"So," Elisha wondered, "did you ever find out what happened to Amy and Crystal? Was I right?"

"Very good theory," Professor Wheeling told her. "We found a concentrated nest of brown wolf hybrids just next to that shaft you explored, and both Amy and Crystal had female pheromone on the clothing in their lockers—and that could have come from scented dollar bills. Amy probably got hers from Jim Boltz. Crystal got hers from—well, who knows? Dollar bills circulate around, from person to person. The scent was all over the school by the time you went down that shaft. Amy and Crystal were only the first ones to be bitten by hybrids. There would have been hundreds more if the spiders hadn't been stopped."

Elisha's gaze fell. "So, it's kind of a good ending, I guess. But it's hard to feel happy about anything. No one should have died. It just didn't have to happen."

"Oh, but there's still one consolation," said Sarah. "There are some students—now on their way to a full recovery—who have a whole new perspective on harassing others."

Her eyes brightened. "The, the other guys? Jim Boltz, and Doug Anderson, and . . ."

"They're going to make it."

"I am so glad!"

"So all the news isn't bad."

"But what about Shawna Miller and Blake Hornsby? Why didn't they get sick?"

"Call it luck, or call it providence. Norman put the wrong spider in Blake's locker, so he was never bitten. As for Shawna, well, the witches put the hex symbol on her locker, but we still got there before Norman did. She's been a much nicer girl now that she realizes how close she came to being a victim."

Elijah said, "You ought to see the high school. They're fumigating the whole thing. Ms. Wyrthen and Mr. Loman are even helping supervise."

"Then it should go very efficiently." They all laughed at that. "Dad? Have you written your report to Mr. Morgan yet?"

He smiled at her. "I was waiting to hear your comments. What would you like to say?" He took out his pocket recorder and clicked it on.

"Well . . ." She thought for a moment. "This may sound kind of strange, but the first thing I want to do is tell Susie Peterson I'm sorry I teased her at Bible camp last summer." Emotion she didn't expect rose within her and her eyes filled with tears. "And I'm sorry I didn't let Ingrid what's-her-name play with me in the second grade. I'm sorry for anybody I've ever hurt."

That made Elijah think of someone. "I need to apologize to Shawn McLindon. I made fun of his guitar playing, but really, he's a lot better than I am."

Elisha continued, "People are precious, and sometimes we forget that. They're precious because God made them, and they need friends, they need love. Jesus never teased or hurt anyone, but He loved everybody, even the little and dumb and fat and ugly and weird, and, well, if we all lived like that, then maybe terrible things like we've just seen wouldn't happen." She feebly wiped a tear from her eye. "And, I guess that's it."

⚬⚬

". . . the doctors tell us it could take another week for the poison to completely purge from her system. After that, Elisha should recover the full use of her limbs and be able to walk again. So we wait at her bedside, prayers of thanksgiving ever on our lips for our brave daughter, and deep gratitude in our hearts for the commitment and heroism of Dr. Algernon Wheeling, Dr. Stuart, and the fine staff at Baker General Hospital."

Sitting before his computer aboard the Holy Roller, parked in the hospital parking lot not far from Elisha's window, Nate Springfield completed his report to Mr. Morgan.

"As we close this investigation, we are sternly warned that the Truth behind the Facts runs far deeper than the commission of the crime itself, the bizarre weapons used, and even the motive. There is a vital lesson to be learned here, a Truth our society must not lose sight of, and that is **the sanctity of every human life and the dignity of every individual.** Increasingly, in a world that seeks to establish its own knowledge and values without God, we find our concept of humanity—real, genuine, *human* humanity—falling through the cracks. If, as our children are so often taught, we are nothing but a cosmic accident that arose for no reason out of primordial slime, and that the *stronger* among us are necessarily the *better* among us, then where does love fit in, or kindness to those in need, or simply going out of our way to lend a hand to a fellow human being? Where will we find heroes who are willing to risk their own comfort and safety, even their very lives, for those who are weaker than they? How do we know there is such a thing as human dignity, or even the simple right to walk through a school hallway without being shoved, beaten, teased, or harassed?

"Metal detectors may keep weapons out of the schools, and security officers can maintain at least a surface tranquillity, but these will not keep out the pain, anger, and loneliness that cause a child to bring a weapon to school in the first place. Unless our children are regularly and emphatically taught respect for themselves and one another *and* provided with a firm and lasting reason for such respect—I suggest, of course, a biblical, godly reason: We are all made in the image of God and are each precious in His sight, regardless of how we look, or what we can do—we have not learned from the incident in Baker, Washington.

"From her hospital bed, my daughter, Elisha, summed it up very well, and her words are worth repeating: 'People are precious, and sometimes we forget that . . .'"

ॐ

In his office in Washington, D.C., Mr. Morgan read the words aloud to his secretary, Consuela, the moment Nate Springfield's final draft came over the fax machine. "'They're precious because God made them, and they need friends, they need love. Jesus never teased or hurt anyone, but He loved everybody, even the little and dumb and fat and ugly and weird, and if we all lived like that, then maybe terrible things like we've just seen wouldn't happen.'"

Consuela wiped a tear from her eye. "If only . . ."

Mr. Morgan nodded. "If only." He eyed the report again and smiled proudly. "I think I'll take it to the President myself." With a pleased chuckle, he gave the pages a proud tap of his hand. "*Veritas!*" he declared and went into his office to get his coat.

FRANK PERETTI

Of all the demons he's written about, this one is anything but fiction.

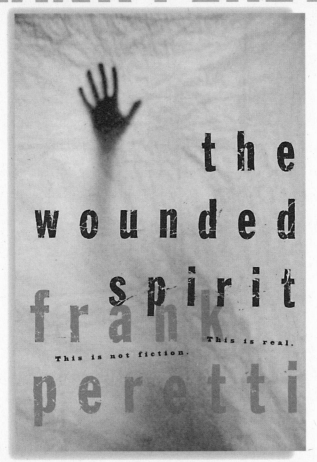

the wounded spirit
frank peretti

This is not fiction.   This is real.

Fact is infinitely more disturbing than fiction.

What drives a person to do the unthinkable? In Frank Peretti's first non-fiction work, he examines the pain from his past and helps us uncover the scars in our own lives. Drawing from tragic news stories—like Columbine—he illustrates how such ridicule and rejection push people beyond the brink. Then with poignant insight, Frank Peretti shows us the way to heal the wounded spirit that actually lies within us all.

Ⓦ WORD PUBLISHING
www.wordpublishing.com   www.thewoundedspirit.com